"You Are [...] Document, A [...] Cameron?"

He had no reason to deny her his signature. Surely he didn't want the responsibility of a ten-month-old baby.

"What will happen if I don't?"

A child's world, and Jo's, would collapse again. "You will."

"What will happen if I do?"

"I'll leave. I promise never to darken your doorstep again."

A slow smile revealed straight white teeth. "Then I'm going to take every possible minute I've got." He leaned right into her ear and whispered, "And you'd like my doorstep. You're welcome to darken it anytime."

Every feminine cell in her body betrayed her, dancing to attention and making her tingle. The very thought of what he was suggesting made her legs feel a little weak. Great. *Just great, Jo.* She hadn't counted on having to fight *herself* to get what she wanted.

Dear Reader,

Thank you for choosing Silhouette Desire. As always, we have a fabulous array of stories for you to enjoy, starting with *Just a Taste* by Bronwyn Jameson, the latest installment in our DYNASTIES: THE ASHTONS continuity series. This tale of forbidden attraction between two romance-wary souls will leave you breathless and wanting more from this wonderful author—who will have a brand-new miniseries of her own, PRINCES OF THE OUTBACK, out later this year.

The terrific Annette Broadrick is back with another book in her CRENSHAWS OF TEXAS series. *Double Identity* is an engrossing page-turner about seduction and lies...you know, all that good stuff! Susan Crosby continues her BEHIND CLOSED DOORS series with *Rules of Attraction*, the first of three brand-new stories set in the world of very private investigations. Roxanne St. Claire brings us a fabulous McGrath brother hero caught in an unexpected situation, in *When the Earth Moves*. Rochelle Alers's THE BLACKSTONES OF VIRGINIA series wraps up with *Beyond Business*, a story in which the Blackstone patriarch gets involved in a surprise romance with his new—and very pregnant—assistant. And last but certainly not least, the engaging Amy Jo Cousins is back this month with *Sleeping Arrangements*, a terms-of-the-will story not to be missed.

Here's hoping you enjoy all six of our selections this month. And, in the months to come, look for Maureen Child's THREE-WAY WAGER series and a brand-new installment of our infamous TEXAS CATTLEMAN'S CLUB.

Happy reading!

Melissa Jeglinski

Melissa Jeglinski
Senior Editor
Silhouette Desire

Please address questions and book requests to:
Silhouette Reader Service
U.S.: 3010 Walden Ave., P.O. Box 1325, Buffalo, NY 14269
Canadian: P.O. Box 609, Fort Erie, Ont. L2A 5X3

When the Earth Moves

ROXANNE ST. CLAIRE

Silhouette® Desire

Published by Silhouette Books

America's Publisher of Contemporary Romance

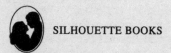 SILHOUETTE BOOKS

ISBN 0-373-76648-3

WHEN THE EARTH MOVES

Visit Silhouette Books at www.eHarlequin.com

Printed in U.S.A.

ROXANNE ST. CLAIRE

began writing romance fiction in 1999 after nearly two decades as a public relations and marketing executive. Retiring from business to pursue a lifelong dream of writing romance is one of the most rewarding accomplishments in her life. The others are her happy marriage to a real-life hero and the daily joys of raising two young children. Roxanne writes mainstream romantic suspense, contemporary romance and women's fiction. Her work has received numerous awards, including the prestigious Heart to Heart Award, the Golden Opportunity Award and the Gateway Award. An active member of the Romance Writers of America, Roxanne lives in Florida and currently writes—and raises children—full-time. She loves to hear from readers through e-mail at roxannestc@aol.com and snail mail at P.O. Box 372909, Satellite Beach, FL 32937. Visit her Web site at www.roxannestclaire.com.

While writing this book, I had the opportunity to "meet" a group of talented, spirited writers who participated in an eHarlequin.com Writing Round Robin. The project was designed for me to teach about craft and encourage aspiring writers…but I was the one who learned, and discovered a source of constant support and friendship.

This book is dedicated to the gang in the Hood, with much love and loyalty.

One

Cameron McGrath never missed the first pitch of a Yankee game. He considered it low class, bad luck and downright disrespectful to a near-holy tradition. So when the receptionist announced that a woman waited in the main lobby of Futura Investments and insisted on seeing him, he swallowed a colorful curse.

"I don't have any more appointments today, Jen." To be certain, he flipped open his PDA and checked the calendar. Of course he wouldn't schedule anything past six on a game night. Especially when the Yankees were playing Boston. "Who's she with?"

"Uh, she's alone."

He smiled, and silently forgave the young girl's mistake. Jen had personality and charm, and that's why she was out front. "Did she say what company she's with? One of our clients? Or is it some kind of sales call?"

No doubt it was. Since he'd taken over as the top attorney at Futura Investments, it seemed he spent far too little time practicing law and way too much time overseeing the legal department. He hadn't gotten dual graduate degrees in law and business to baby-sit junior lawyers and make decisions on office equipment, although it seemed he'd done a lot of both lately.

"She's not with any company, Mr. McGrath." The receptionist lowered her voice. "I think this is *personal*. I mean—she looks like someone, like maybe she's…she looks personal."

Personal? Amanda? She could be relentless when ignored. It had only been a week since he'd called her— or was it two? Geez. He'd been perfectly honest from the beginning of their short relationship, but that didn't stop any marriage-starved Manhattan woman who had her sights set on a new last name. *His.*

He glanced at his watch. He'd take her along to the game. At least he wouldn't be late and she'd count it as a date. "Tell her I'll be out in a minute. Hope she's dressed for a game."

Jen's laugh sounded more like surprise than humor. "I guess it depends on what you're playing."

With Amanda, he'd place his bets on a short leather skirt, a skimpy but painfully expensive top, and heels as high as the Chrysler Building. He smiled. She could be relentless, all right. And sometimes that worked in everyone's favor.

The smile was still on his face as he loosened his tie and turned the corner toward the Futura lobby, ready to greet the former model he'd met at a fund-raiser two months earlier.

But as he glanced through the glass doors of the reception area, he froze midstep and slack-jawed.

That was *not* Amanda.

She stood with her back to him, studying the panoramic city view out the floor-to-ceiling windows. A pair of worn, faded jeans hugged a heart-shaped backside, with one cowboy-booted foot tapping the carpet, either in impatience or to a tune that played in her head. A thick mane of reddish-brown hair covered most of her back, just about kissing the top of those sinful-looking jeans. And on her head she wore a black cowboy hat.

She looked like one long, lean, bull-riding machine.

Did he know this woman?

As he opened the lobby door, she slowly turned, tipped her hat back on her forehead and answered that question with one heart-stopping gaze. Nope. He would never have forgotten that face. Wide-set eyes the color of copper pennies, buttercream skin and a mouth that demanded hours of close scrutiny.

And, he noticed with a bit of surprise, not a speck of makeup. He'd never even *seen* Amanda without makeup—or at least the remnants of it.

"Mr. McGrath?" She took a few quick strides toward him, the sound of her boot heels on the marble floor echoing the beat of his increased pulse rate.

"I'm Cam McGrath." He extended a hand in greeting. "Can I…" *Help?* No, help was not on the list of things he wanted to do to and for her.

"Jo Ellen Tremaine." Her handshake was solid, but her gaze held a question, a sense of anticipation. Was he supposed to recognize her name? Was she opposing counsel on a Futura case? He was drawing a blank. Or maybe that was because his brain cells had shut down in deference to an alternative organ.

He forced himself to focus on her face, but she hoisted a tote bag over her shoulder, the action pulling her shirt a little to the side and revealing the translucent skin of her throat and collarbone.

"I know you're off to a meeting," she said. "So I won't take but a second of your time."

"No problem. It's nothing urgent." Had he just told her the Yankees and Red Sox were not urgent? He had to get a grip. Pretty women could be found on every street in New York. They just didn't generally dress for the rodeo. "What can I do for you?"

She glanced toward Jen, who hadn't missed one second of the brief interplay. "Could I speak with you privately?"

He weighed his options. Spend some time talking to this gorgeous cowgirl. Be late for the Yankees. Cowgirl. Yankees.

"My office is right down the hall." He tilted his head toward the door in invitation.

She took off her hat and shook out her hair, causing some silky strands to fall over her shoulders. His gaze dropped to her pale-blue button-down shirt, complete with silver snaps.

Yeehaw.

Holding the door, he managed a good long look at the fitted back pockets of her jeans again. The Yankees would play at home eighty-one times this season. A jaw-dropping version of Dale Evans would only appear in his office once. He had definitely made the right choice.

"Can I offer you something to drink, Ms. Tremaine?" he asked as they entered his office and he closed the door.

"You can call me Jo. And unless you have an ice-cold Bud on tap, I'm fine."

He chuckled a little. "Wouldn't you know it? My office tap is out." He suddenly remembered the six-pack of Amber Bock in his refrigerator at home. Intended for

Saturday's softball game, but easily replaced. "Or we could go somewhere else."

"No, thanks." She stood in the middle of the room, her gaze direct and unwavering. "This won't take that long. I hope."

He heard an infinitesimal catch in her voice, something only a lawyer trained to sniff out half-truths and cover-ups would notice.

He gestured toward the sofa in the sitting area of his office. "Please. Have a seat."

She folded herself into one of the chairs, her faded denim and black boots looking oddly out of place on the chrome-and-leather divan he'd had designed when he took over the massive corner office.

"Are you from around here…Jo?" The name suited her. She wasn't feminine. Womanly, oh, yeah. But nothing fluttered in her movements, not her fingers, not her eyelashes. Jo. He liked it.

"I'm from Sierra Springs, California."

He inched back in surprise.

"Have you heard of it?" She sounded like she expected him to say yes.

"I can't say that I have, but you've come a long way. Is Sierra Springs near the Silicon Valley?" They had clients out there, several of them. This had to be related to Futura somehow.

She shook her head, smoothing her jeans with one long, slow stroke of her hands, a whisper of a cynical smile tipping her lips. "Not *that* valley. Sierra Springs is on the border between California and Nevada, a hundred miles from Sacramento, in the foothills of the Sierra Nevada mountains."

His knowledge of the area geography was scarce, at best. No clients that he could think of. No potential investments. Not much of anything but the Ponderosa Ranch and some second-class gambling in Reno. "Pretty quiet up there, I bet."

"It was. Until the earth shook us down to our boots and rattled our brains into scrambled eggs."

"The earth?" He zipped through a mental hard drive. What was she talking about? "Oh, yes." He snapped his fingers and pointed at her. "I have heard of Sierra Springs. There was an earthquake there a few months ago. A big one."

She nodded. "Five point six. And some nasty after-shocks."

This was definitely a lawsuit waiting to happen. "Five point six, whoa. That is major. Did it affect—were you hit hard?"

His gaze traveled over those jean-clad legs again, hoping against hope that whatever her business they wouldn't be adversaries. He'd very much prefer to counsel her. Among other things.

She shrugged. "I lost some...people."

Staff? Family? Whoever, he had no doubt that her loss was at the root of this unorthodox meeting.

"I'm sorry to hear that." He seemed to recall five people died at one site. An apartment building. And then the image of a firefighter carrying a one-year-old from a hellhole of debris flashed in his mind. Of course—the *baby* found in the rubble. The story had been on every news station for days.

Did she own the building? Did *Futura?* Surely he'd have been briefed on that kind of potential lawsuit if they did.

"So, what do you do in Sierra Springs?" With some witnesses, the most innocuous questions cut right to the truth. He half imagined she'd say she roped horses and cattle, but more likely, she was another lawyer. They just dressed differently in California.

"I do body work."

His pulse kicked up again. "Excuse me?"

"Car repairs. Wrecks."

"You're a mechanic?"

"I'm a collision repair expert." A little light danced in her bronze-brown eyes as she narrowed them. "I own my own body shop."

"Really." So she wasn't a rodeo queen *or* a lawyer. She pounded steel for a living.

Without thinking, his gaze slid back to her hands, long and slender and not a grease stain on them. And free of any jewelry—not even a single gold band. "Well you've certainly piqued my curiosity, Ms.—Jo. What brings you to New York?"

"You."

His body tightened with a low, natural response to the single raspy word.

"Me?" Okay. Don't look a gift horse in the mouth. Even if that mouth is damn near edible. "How's that?"

"I need you to sign a paper."

Legal alarms sounded in the back of his head. "What kind of a paper?"

"It's called a Petition of Relinquishment and Consent."

He thought for a minute, his mind skimming first-year law. "Isn't that part of the adoption process?"

For a moment she didn't move. The tip of her tongue peeked through her unadorned lips and dampened them. "Yes."

"I don't understand. Why would you need my signature?"

"I'm in the process of adopting a baby. And she is a…distant relative of yours."

He leaned forward as though she pulled him on a string. "A relative of mine?"

"She's your…your niece."

He shook his head. "I don't have a niece. I have two brothers and neither one has children." Unease trickled through his veins, but he dismissed it. If Colin or Quinn had fathered a baby, he'd know it. They had no secrets, nothing they didn't share with one another. Could this be a ploy for money? A hoax? "I think you've made a mistake. Who is the child?"

"There's no mistake," she insisted. "She's definitely your niece."

"I'm utterly certain I don't have a niece."

She raised one beautifully shaped brow. "Don't be utterly anything until you've heard the facts."

Objection sustained. "Who is the father?"

"Her father's entirely out of the picture, and anyway, he's not related to you. It's her mother. Her mother is—was—a woman by the name of Katie McGrath."

As if he had a Rolodex in his mind's eye, he flipped through every distant McGrath cousin he could remember. No Katie. "I've never heard of her."

Slowly she crossed and uncrossed her legs. "No, you wouldn't have. You've never met her. But her mother is Christine McGrath."

His gut squeezed into a knot.

"And that is your mother," she said calmly. "So Katie is your sister. Or was. On both counts, I'm sorry to say."

"No. I couldn't have a—" He was speechless.

He couldn't have a sister? Of course he could. An odd numbness began to make his arms and legs ache. He recognized the sensation. He'd first felt it when he was nine years old, the day he watched his mom climb in a station wagon and drive away, leaving a husband and three sons forever.

But he'd gotten so very, very good at making that ache go away. Sheer mind-over-body control was all it took, and if Cam was good at anything, it was control.

Her words replayed. *Katie is your sister. Or was. On both counts…* "Where is my—Christine McGrath?"

"I'm afraid she and Katie were both casualties in the earthquake."

He waited for a rush of emotion, but nothing came. No surprise there. He'd killed any feelings for his mother years ago. He felt Jo's gaze locked on him, waiting for a response. "Sorry to hear that, but I have no relationship with my mother. If this is the same woman who—I really have no connection with her *whatsoever.*" He wanted his point to be crystal clear.

"Then it shouldn't be any problem *whatsoever* to sign this paper," she said, pulling an envelope from her oversize handbag.

"Whoa. Wait a second, there." He held his hand up. "I'm a lawyer. We don't sign anything."

"If you need proof that she was your mother, I have it. I expected you'd want to see that."

He stared at her, trying to fit the jigsaw puzzle together. Slowly, he reached for the envelope.

"Christine McGrath left our home twenty-six years ago and moved to Wyoming," he said, slowly opening the paper.

"No. She didn't." At his sharp look, she clarified, "Move to Wyoming, that is."

According to his father, she had, and none of the McGrath boys had had reason to question him. Not that discussion of his mother's whereabouts was dinner conversation at their house.

She squared her shoulders and regarded him with the bracing gaze of a judge about to hand down a harsh sentence. "She went to Sierra Springs twenty-six years ago, had a child named Katie and, eleven months ago, Katie had a baby. Callie McGrath."

His throat closed up, and his fingers froze on the unopened paper. Was this possible?

"I'm going to adopt Callie, Mr. McGrath. But I can't do that until her closest living relative signs this document and relinquishes any rights to her. I can't spend the rest of my life worrying if you'll show up and want custody of her."

Want custody? Of a *baby?* "Sweetheart, I don't want custody of a *goldfish.*"

"Great." She stood quickly, tapped her hat back in place and nodded toward the paper in his hand. "All you have to do is sign it and you'll never see me again. I can assure you of that."

Part of him wanted to do just that. The part that always crushed any memories of his mother, the part that taught him years ago to have complete control over his environment, his life, his emotions.

But another part heard a nagging little voice that he really would have liked to ignore. But he couldn't.

You're going to heal the hurt in this family, Cam Mc-Grath. His grandmother's Irish lilt was as clear in his head as the first time she made her pronouncement. *You're the oldest. It's your job. You'll heal the hurt.*

He'd forgotten that prediction. Just as he and Colin and Quinn had forgotten the *hurt.* Or learned to fake that they had.

But here stood a woman with the answers all of them had secretly craved for twenty-six years. The answers that might make three McGrath men finally, once and for all, close the holes that had busted wide open in their hearts so many years ago. The answers that might rid them of the memory of the day they'd crouched at a second-story window and watched their mother blow out of Pittsburgh. For Wyoming. Or California. Or *some*where.

Evidently, he had to make another choice tonight. And the recriminations could be far worse than missing the first few innings of a baseball game.

He could sign the paper and forget Jo Ellen Tremaine ever graced his office. Or he could get some answers from the cowgirl mechanic.

This could be his only chance to *heal the hurt*—for Gram McGrath, and for his brothers.

He would just never, ever let this woman know that's what he was doing.

He stood and gave her a slow, lazy grin. "So, Jo. Do you like baseball, by any chance?"

Jo resisted the urge to let her jaw drop. Cameron McGrath stood a full six foot something and gazed down at her with what could only be called a glint in deep-blue eyes.

Baseball? Was he serious?

"I think it's dull as dirt," she replied.

The glint disappeared and the eyes narrowed to disbelieving slits, feathered with eyelashes that, she couldn't help noticing, were just as long and thick as Katie's had been. "Dull as *dirt?*"

Did he really want to discuss the merits of baseball four minutes after she told him his long-lost sister and mother had recently *died* and that he had a baby niece whom she planned to adopt? Could he be *that* cold?

Of course he could. Jo had read the letters from Katie's mother to this man's father. The letters he'd sent back with a scratchy "Return to Sender" note on the front. Jim McGrath had vinegar in his veins and evidently, that blood type was dominant on the McGrath side. Katie had missed the bad blood, but obviously got the traffic-stopping good looks.

This McGrath, however, had slightly different coloring from his sister. His hair was dark blond, his eyes the color of the September sky on a clear California day. He was rugged, with a shadow of beard and thick eyebrows. Still, he had the wide-set eyes, the chiseled jaw, the perfect cheekbones—features universal in beautiful people and in McGraths.

From what she could surmise under his gazillion-dollar, custom-made, three-button designer suit, he had a flawless body, too.

She forced her attention to the reason she came to New York: the envelope in his hand. "How much time do you need to read that and sign it?"

He shrugged, his gaze on her now and not the envelope. Assessing, scrutinizing. "I'm not sure. How much time do you think it'll take to change your mind about the nation's pastime?"

She almost laughed at how shallow he sounded. "You don't have that much time, Mr. McGrath. I'm leaving on a red-eye at eleven-thirty." *With that piece of paper, signed, in my hand.*

He made a show of looking at a sleek timepiece on his wrist. "If we're lucky, we'll make the bottom of the first. And—" he looked back at her and winked "—with no extra innings, you might get to see the whole game."

Shallow *and* cocky. One of her least favorite combinations, no matter how well packaged. "I'm not going to any baseball games tonight. But the sooner you sign that paper, the sooner you can get to the park."

"Not the park. The Stadium," he corrected. "With a capital *S*."

She managed a rueful smile. What would she have to do to get that petition signed?

"I'm guessing this is pretty important to you," he finally said, leaning just close enough for her to catch a whiff of a musky, male scent.

His baritone assumption held enough of a challenge to send pings of apprehension dancing down her spine. Or maybe those were pings of...something else. She'd have to be blind, deaf and neutered not to recognize the raw attractiveness of this man. But she'd have to be stupid to let that influence her.

She wasn't neutered or stupid, only determined. Callie McGrath would not become a ward of the state, or some kind of novelty for curious, distant, icy family members. Jo Ellen might not be the model of maternal instinct, but she couldn't resist repairing a wreck. And Katie had left one hell of a mess when she died with no will and no plan for her tiny baby.

She phrased her response carefully. "Yes, it's important. Important that it's done right. I don't want any loose ends threatening to strangle me."

A half smile tipped the corners of his lips. "I don't want to strangle you, sweetheart. Just share a little dull-as-dirt baseball with you. And during the game—" he put a warm hand on her shoulder "—we can get to know each other a little bit."

She heard the subtle message in the request. He was a lawyer, as he'd made sure to remind her. And he wasn't about to hand his signature and consent to a complete stranger.

"Fair enough," she agreed, dipping out of his touch. "But is it absolutely necessary to go to a baseball game?"

"Absolutely." He laughed a little and inched her toward the door. "Plus you can have that beer."

She had a feeling she'd need it.

Two

Cameron watched her climb into the back seat of a cab, admiring both her spontaneity—however reluctant—and the delicate curve of her rear end. He'd decided moments after she dropped her little bombshell exactly how he'd play this game. The only way he played anything. Cool.

First of all, she could have the wrong Christine McGrath. Or she could be some sort of con artist. Or she could be a total fruitcake.

But on the off chance she was telling the truth, he'd give her a shot. Spending the evening with her wouldn't be a hardship. Playing it cool was easy enough, since the news of his mother's death didn't have the usual effect it would on most men—but then, Christine McGrath hadn't acted like most men's mother. And the fact that he had a surprise sister who had also perished in an act of nature was a miserable shame, but he had no control over that.

If he had known Katie even existed… An unfamiliar pressure constricted his chest. He hadn't known. Period. He couldn't control that, either.

And Cameron avoided anything he couldn't control. So he'd avoid any regret that accompanied the thought that a girl, a girl who had shared at least half his gene pool, had lived and breathed and, sadly, died. As far as the baby—well, that was a no-brainer. He certainly didn't want a child.

Of course, he had two brothers. But Quinn had just gotten married, and he and Nicole were up to their eyeballs restoring their resort in Florida. Colin was planning his wedding to Grace, and they were also consumed with their new architectural firm and huge assignment that had them living in Newport, Rhode Island. He couldn't say for sure, but he doubted either of his brothers were thinking about children—their own or their *sister's.*

And Dad? Well, James McGrath had become a loner in the last few years, retired from his construction business, the job of raising his sons complete. Should he be told of his former wife's passing? Of her daughter's death?

Did *any* of them need to know this? Was this outrageous tale even remotely possible? And why would Jo show up at *his* office and not a different McGrath's?

You'll heal the hurt, Cam McGrath.

He shifted in his seat, which brought him a little closer to the mysterious woman dressed like she owned a ranch instead of a body shop. She sat stone still, staring out the window at the streets of New York City.

She placed her hands flat on her thighs, a position he'd noticed in his office. At the same time, she took a quiet, deep breath and exhaled. She was the picture of serenity.

"So, where'd you learn to be a mechanic?"

She flashed him a vile look. "I'm *not* a mechanic."

"That's good," he replied, placing a friendly hand on top of hers and adding an assuring pat. "I don't trust mechanics."

She picked up his hand and removed it from hers. "I don't trust lawyers."

He laughed. "But you didn't answer my question. How does one train to be a...collision repair expert?"

"Trade school. I apprenticed in Sacramento for a while, then worked in Reno. We opened the shop about a year ago."

We? His gaze instinctively dropped back to that unadorned left hand. "Is your husband in the same business?"

"I don't have a husband."

Another earthquake casualty? "Ah. I just assumed when you said 'we' that you meant you and your husband."

"You assumed wrong." This time a smile teased the corner of her lips. "The *we* was Katie and me. She was my business partner."

"My sister worked in a body shop?" He couldn't keep the surprise out of his voice.

She plucked an imaginary thread from her jeans, her smile threatening to get wider. "I can't let you go one minute believing that." She looked up, a hint of mirth sparkling like gold dust in her eyes. "She couldn't bear to set a pedicured foot in the work bay, and the sound of a sander sent her running with her hands clamped over her ears."

He wasn't sure he liked that, either. It was unimaginable for a McGrath—male or female—to act like a sissy. "But she was your partner."

"She was my *business* partner. But we had two separate businesses in the same building, under the same corporate name. Buff 'n' Fluff."

A hearty laugh escaped before he could stop it. "Buff 'n' Fluff? What kind of business is that?"

She shrugged, as though she'd heard the question a million times before. "Auto body repair is Buff—a common term for a metal rough out. And Fluff is a beauty salon." She feathered her own hair with two fingers, some auburn locks fluttering over her shoulder. "Fluff, like blow dry. It's a cosmetology term. That was Katie's end of the business."

"She was a hairstylist," he noted, an image of a woman slowly taking shape in his brain. An image he didn't want to have.

"She was a cosmetologist," Jo corrected. "Hair, face, nails. Anything related to beauty—that was her specialty."

Cam tried to erase the vague sense of a female version of his dark-haired younger brothers, but he couldn't. The vision had taken hold. Damn. He'd really rather not dwell on a person he'd never meet.

"So I take it you've never been to a professional baseball game before."

She turned her head toward him at the sudden topic shift. "Our business sponsored the Sierra Springs Little League last year. Does that count?"

He laughed again. "No wonder you thought it was dull as dirt." The comment still smarted. How could anyone not see the poetry in baseball? He supposed someone who banged fenders for a living might overlook the elegance of a well-turned double play. "This is a little different. This is Yankee Stadium. It's the Mecca of all baseball."

"If you say so," she agreed slowly, her little bit of a Western twang delighting his ear. "Seems like a lot doesn't happen for nine innings, then all of a sudden hell breaks loose and ten runs come in and it's over. Then someone's crying."

He chuckled again, her description of a Little League game bringing back a whole bunch of memories. "Haven't you ever heard? There's no crying in baseball."

"Whoever said that never saw an eight-year-old get his front end walloped with a hard ball," she said, looking out the window again. After a second, she turned back to him, a questioning expression on her face. "Would you like to know about your mother?" she asked quietly.

He regarded her for a long time, vaguely aware that there just wasn't enough air in the closed-in cab. Her gaze was demanding, her lips slightly parted as she waited for his response.

He leaned in enough to almost feel her warm breath near his mouth. She didn't move.

"No." With one finger, he tapped the shadow of a cleft in her chin. "Would you like to know where our seats are?"

She raised that gorgeously arched eyebrow again but didn't move. "No. I'll just be surprised."

"Pleasantly," he promised, backing away to give her a little breathing space. He'd made his point.

"Did you bring that envelope?" she asked.

He patted the pocket of his suit jacket. "Yep."

"Good. I need to get to the airport in time to make my flight. And I expect to have it with me."

And she'd made her point, as well.

This could be a very close game tonight.

When the cabbie dropped them off at a busy street corner, they stood in the shadow of a massive structure.

The streets around them teemed with people and hummed with energy.

How the blazes did this happen, Jo thought with a flash of panic? *Yankee Stadium* wasn't in her plan.

Ever since Mother Earth had caused a seismic shift in Jo's priorities, her plan was to adopt the child she already loved. She'd assumed it would be simple. Callie's father had long before relinquished parental rights, wanting to hide from the fact that he was a married weasel who made promises to Katie he'd never keep.

And for a while, everything progressed smoothly. She'd waded through a sea of endless paperwork, passed the prodding interviews, charmed the Child Services bureaucrats, restructured her shop, her home, her very life. Until Jo's mother sat her down and broke the story of Aunt Chris's secret life before she'd come to Sierra Springs.

Stunned and saddened, but undeterred, Jo had spent hours quite literally digging through the debris that was Christine McGrath's life. And more hours slogging through the Internet for information on her sons, then wrestling with what was the appropriate, safest, *right* course of action.

In the end she was sure she knew what that was. Katie was gone, and so was the woman Jo grew up calling "Aunt" Chris. But somehow, for some reason, an infant had survived nature's rumbling fury, and Jo was willing to do absolutely anything to be sure Callie was safe and protected and loved.

Even make a side trip to Yankee Stadium.

She stole a look at the man who'd brought her to said stadium. His preoccupation with baseball in the midst of a family crisis confirmed that Cameron McGrath was as unfeeling and uncaring as his father, who had forced his pregnant wife out of the house. A man who would be repelled by the idea of being saddled with someone else's *mistake*. That's why she picked *this* brother to approach with the papers. Amid news reports of his business success, she'd seen a pattern of brief romances with socialites, increasing her expectations that Cameron would be most like the man who'd cast out Christine. True, the fact that he was a lawyer unnerved her. But more important, he was the *unattached* McGrath brother, so he'd be the least likely to want a baby. And as the oldest, she hoped his signature would carry the most legal weight.

So far he'd done a fine imitation of unfeeling. Refusing to discuss his mother. Changing the subject. Not even asking how Callie had survived the earthquake. Dragging Jo through New York. Even flirting with her. But she sensed something under his smooth, polished surface. Something so powerful that it qualified as the polar opposite of unfeeling.

Until she knew what feelings he hid, it wouldn't kill her to pretend to like baseball.

"This…" he interrupted her thoughts with a grand gesture toward the mountain of concrete stadium in front of them, "is the House that Ruth Built."

Next to where they stood was a three-story-high replica of a baseball bat. She set her hat back to get a good look at it and nodded. *"Mecca."*

He grinned and guided her toward one of the gates. "Don't get me started on statistics and history. I'll bore you to death."

She doubted Cameron McGrath could bore her. He could probably infuriate her, he most certainly could fascinate her, and, Lord, he could surely arouse her if she gave him the chance. The man was a walking powder keg of masculine, seductive energy.

He led her toward a small crowd at one of the gates. The sensation of his hand on the small of her back sent a pool of warmth through her.

He greeted the ticket-taker, and guided her through a turnstile into the stadium. The sounds and smells of early summer evaporated as they entered what felt like the interior of a giant cement whale, replaced by a medley of foreign scents and noises. The entire place echoed with the din of raised voices and the clatter of feet on concrete. Without thinking, she took Cameron's hand as he bounded through the labyrinth of horizontal ramps, his confident steps energized by an air of familiarity and a sense of urgency.

He paused long enough to listen to the muffled words of an announcer. "We're up. Bottom of the first. Let's go."

He tugged at her hand and she had to stretch her stride to keep up with him, ignoring the vendors' pleas for them to buy hot dogs, nachos or peanuts. She tucked her hat under her arm so it didn't sail off in their wake, and inhaled the overpowering scent of grilled meat and onions. She hadn't eaten all day, and the aroma made her mouth water.

But her overloaded senses obliterated the hunger. Sudden bursts of cheers and applause, flashes of blinding light and green grass through tunnels that led to the field, and the unnervingly comforting sensation of holding his hand all managed to make her a little dizzy.

Dizzy? What the heck was that all about? She hammered steel into submission for a living. She hiked mile-high mountains for fun. She was the original tough chick. How could one foray into Yankee Stadium on the arm of some maniacal fan make her dizzy? It had to be the documents that he held in his jacket pocket, the importance of her mission.

Somehow she had to get through this game and get his signature. Then she'd tear off to the airport and fly home to Callie. With her mission accomplished.

"Pray there's no score," he said to her as they approached a uniformed security guard. "It's bad enough to miss the first pitch, but missing a run could kill me."

"Cam, we were worried about you!" The guard held out his hand like a fist and Cameron knuckled it with a similar gesture.

"Eddie, my man. What's goin' on?"

"Three up, three down in the top of the first, and let me tell you Mussina's slider looks friggin' magical." Eddie's nasal New York accent was so thick, Jo had to concentrate to understand him.

"Who's up?" Cameron asked.

"A-Rod."

"Already?" He sounded crushed.

Eddie let out a disgusted snort. "Yeah, they're screwin' with the lineup. Loftin grounded out, and Jeter went down swingin'." His gaze shifted to her, sweeping her up and down with obvious interest. A broad grin blared his approval. "I knew you had to have one helluva good cause to be this late, Cam."

"Eddie, this good cause is Jo Ellen Tremaine. First timer, from California."

Eddie's eyebrows shot up. "California, huh? A's or Angels?"

Hazy angels? "Excuse me?"

Cameron chuckled and put that way too familiar arm around her again. "Oakland A's—Athletics. Or the California Angels. Who do you root for?"

"Sorry." She made an apologetic face. "I don't really follow the sport."

This earned a belly laugh from Eddie and he waved

a finger of warning at her. "Well, you will, or," he pointed to Cameron, "you'll have to kiss your new boyfriend goodbye."

No use trying to correct him. She just shrugged as though the loss of that boyfriend wouldn't matter any more than the loss of a game.

"Let's go, sweetheart." Cameron urged her into a narrow opening toward the lights of the stadium.

She nodded to Eddie, who continued to grin and shake his head, then she turned to face the sea of green in front of her.

It looked like a vast, luxurious emerald carpet textured with symmetrical patterns, bordered in red-brown dirt and surrounded by thousands and thousands of people cheering, hollering, eating, drinking and laughing. She'd been in baseball parks before, but this place had a mix of playfulness, attitude and superiority. Sort of like the man who'd brought her here.

Still holding her hand, Cameron tugged her down a few steps, into a row of box seats not far from the Yankee dugout. First base was close enough that she could see specks of red clay covering the canvas bag. A shower of greetings came at them, and Cameron responded with a series of "Hey" and "How ya doin'?" that included high-fives and more knuckle tapping.

They settled into seats and he dropped a casual arm around her, leaning close to her ear. "You *do* know who A-Rod is, don't you?"

"Yes." The name sounded more like a tool than a person, but he didn't need to know that.

Suddenly a hollow whack propelled the entire stadium to its feet, including her, as Cameron pulled her from her seat and she instinctively squinted up into the blinding lights.

Then everyone moaned and sat down. By the time Jo saw a player in the outfield throw in the ball, they were seated again, too. Cameron's arm took up permanent residence around her shoulders, the distinctive, delicious scent of him overpowering the smell of popcorn and humanity around her.

"You want that beer?" he asked.

She leaned back enough to make sure he could see her warning look. "This isn't a date."

He grinned and threw a quick glance over his shoulder. "Fake it for me, okay? I got a reputation from one end of the Bronx to the other."

"I bet you do."

His gaze locked on hers, way too warm and friendly for the situation they were in. "A good reputation," he assured her. "As a gentleman who would buy a lady anything she wants at the ballpark."

What she wanted was the paper in his pocket. Signed. "I'll have whatever you have."

Another smack of the ball against the bat stole his attention and they were up again. This time the hit was a success, landing the player on second base. Maybe she should at least try to follow the game.

She sat back down, but Cameron remained standing and whistled at a vendor. Peanuts flew at them, followed by the arrival of two foaming plastic cups. More jokes and pronouncements were tossed around among the people who all seemed to know one another, and before Jo really knew what was happening, it was the fourth inning and she'd had half a beer and three-quarters of a bag of peanuts. And she finally understood what a balk was.

But she didn't feel any closer to success.

Cameron talked about his team with a mesmerizing

passion, his movements spare, his expressions intense. His whole body somehow managed to stay practically pressed to her side, the metal arm of the seat the only thing preventing her from feeling the steel of his muscles, the warmth of his substantial frame.

She couldn't help sneaking glances at him while he watched the game. Nor could she help noticing that he did the same. Only there was nothing sneaky about his gazes. He looked at her—a lot, and with great interest—and every time he did, an unwanted response sparked through her whole body.

She tried to keep the conversation light and act as if she didn't notice the undercurrent of tension and attraction between them. For whatever reason, he'd brought her with him. And she would play his game until she got what she wanted.

"How did you become such a Yankee fan?" she asked. "Don't they have a baseball team in Pittsburgh?"

He froze middrink of beer, obviously surprised by the question. They hadn't discussed where he'd grown up.

"New York is my home now," he said simply, then took his sip. "I went to college and law school at Fordham about ten minutes from here, and I got my MBA at Columbia. I live, breathe, eat and root for New York City."

"I know," she said quietly, earning another surprised glance. But she didn't know why he'd virtually abandoned the home of his youth.

"I'm at a distinct disadvantage," he softly announced, so close to her ear that her stomach dipped at the vibrations his voice caused. "You seem to know a lot more about me than I know about you."

He had a right to some information about her, she reminded herself. No harm in that. "I live and work in Sierra Springs. I'm thirty years old, own my own home and run a body shop in town." How personal did he want to get?

"Do you have a boyfriend?"

Very personal. "No."

"Ever been married?"

She supposed it was a legitimate question, considering the pending adoption. "Briefly."

"What happened?"

"He wanted to move to L.A."

"And you couldn't work that little detail out?" He looked dubious, and she swallowed before answering with the truth.

"He wanted to move to L.A. with another woman."

"Oh."

Yeah, oh. She shrugged. "Stuff happens."

"Sure does. How long were you married?"

A collective cheer from the crowd threatened to drown out her response, but he actually stayed seated and waited to hear her answer.

"I was married for about a year," she told him. "I was only twenty-two." She really hadn't expected to have to give him too much personal information, figuring he'd want to know about his sister and mother. And maybe Callie.

She was willing to give Cameron McGrath everything he wanted, any pictures, information—including the letters from his mother to his father—if he would sign the paper. She had documentation right there in her bag. That, and a toothbrush, comb and a change of underwear, was all she'd packed for her one-day round-trip to New York. She had no intention of staying one minute longer than she needed to. The next meeting with Child Services was the following week, and she planned to be prepared.

"No children?" he asked, still on the ancient history of her marriage.

"Just the one I plan on adopting."

Oh Lord, what if her worst nightmare came true? What if he suddenly decided *he* should raise Callie? The thought seemed preposterous from a man who admitted he didn't want the responsibility of a fish, but more preposterous things had happened in the past few months. The law would be on his side, even though his lifestyle didn't exactly welcome a child. Unless he planned to bring a stroller into Yankee Stadium. How could she subtly remind him of that?

"You've never been married," she stated simply.

"Never have, never will."

Relief made her fingers tingle. "You seem sure of that."

A half smile tipped his lips. "Some things are a safe bet, Jo."

"And marriage isn't one of them?"

"That's not what I'm saying." He took another sip of his beer, then set the cup back on the ground. "What's a safe bet is that I'll never get married."

Welcome news, in this case. But how could he be so sure? "Why is that?"

He looked at her the same way he had when she didn't know who played shortstop. "I think you know enough about my personal history to answer that yourself."

She frowned. What was she missing here? "Do you mean because of your parents?"

"Not my parents," he corrected quickly. "My mother. She sort of soured me on lifelong relationships."

His *mother?* She'd been forced to leave and had tried for years to rekindle a relationship with her husband and sons. They'd shunned her. Was it possible...he didn't know that?

The crowd roared again, but he surprised her by pulling her a little closer and pointing toward the field. "Now just look at that, sweetheart," he said with an easy chuckle, his gaze focused on the field. "Tell me there's anything *dull* about that brilliant pickoff."

What was brilliant was his change-of-subject technique. But that was fine. She didn't want to delve into his past if he didn't. The less said about it, the better. However, she didn't want him to go too far off topic.

"I need to get to Kennedy by ten-thirty at the latest," she reminded him.

He glanced at the time on the scoreboard. "That'll be tough."

Her heart squeezed. He couldn't do this. He had no reason to deny her his signature. It was obvious he didn't care about his mother, and surely he didn't want the responsibility of a eleven-month-old baby. "You are going to sign that document, aren't you, Cameron?"

He tightened his hold on her ever so slightly. "What will happen if I don't?"

A child's world, and Jo's, would collapse again. "You will."

"What will happen if I do?"

"I'll leave. I can get a cab myself. I promise never to darken your doorstep again."

A slow smile revealed straight white teeth. "Then I'm going to take every possible minute I've got." He leaned right into her ear and whispered, "And you'd like my doorstep. It's in a great part of town and professionally decorated. You're welcome to darken it anytime."

Every feminine cell in her body betrayed her, dancing to attention and making her tingle. The very thought of what he was suggesting made her legs feel a little weak. Great. *Just great, Jo.* She hadn't counted on having to fight *herself* to get what she wanted.

She tried the deep-breathing technique Katie had taught her when she was in her yoga phase, but it came out like an anxious shudder, and his grin widened at the sound.

"Don't be nervous," he said with a soft laugh, patting her thigh just intimately enough to leave an imaginary burn mark. "We're only down by one. And the Sox are cursed…usually. You've got nothing to worry about."

They both knew she wasn't worried about the game.

Three

The seventh inning was a killer. Boston scored four runs, and the Yanks needed not one but two pitching changes. Things didn't look good.

At the stretch, it was past nine-thirty. Cam knew they'd never see the end of the game if he was going to get Jo to the airport for an eleven-thirty flight to the West Coast.

Anyway, the Yankees were so deep into the bullpen that this one might be a goner. He still had questions. A lot of questions.

Not that he really gave a rat's ass what happened to Christine McGrath. But his brothers had just been babies when she drove off like Thelma without Louise. They had a right to know. Especially Colin. Cam's youngest brother had always blamed himself for their mother's abandonment, but the little monster had been barely old enough to say his own name when she'd disappeared. He owed the information to Colin, and to Quinn.

He took Jo's hand and squeezed it, liking any excuse to touch her. "It's time to go," he said softly.

Her coppery eyes lit with surprise, then she frowned. "You want to stay for the bottom of this inning, don't you?"

It was his turn to be surprised—that she'd even make the offer. "Yeah. But I'd rather you didn't stomp me with one of your cowboy boots for missing your flight."

They stood, he said his goodbyes to all the box neighbors he spent so many nights with every summer, and he walked her toward the tunnel.

He heard the crack of the bat behind him, knowing by the sound of the crowd that it was a line drive. When he didn't pause, she looked up at him expectantly.

He gave her a sly grin. "You really don't think I'd let you be late, do you?" The announcer called a double. Double *damn*.

Slipping her arm through his, she rewarded him with a million-dollar smile. "Thank you, Cam."

Aw, hell. That smile was worth missing a grand slam. "No problem. As long as you're willing to admit the truth now."

Her step slowed. "The truth?"

He pointed a thumb over his shoulder toward the field. "Dull as dirt?"

"Well…" She dragged out the word and squeezed his arm, the intimacy of the gesture hitting him like a blast of heat. "Your enthusiasm could be contagious."

He laughed and pulled her closer, noting that her step seemed to lighten and her smile seemed genuine. She could sense she was getting what she came for, and that obviously made her very happy.

"You know, Jo," he said as they left the stadium and

stepped onto the streets of the Bronx, "I gotta tell you something."

"What?"

Maybe it was the elusive, clean fragrance of her hair, or the feel of her slender arm wrapped through his. Maybe it was the odd companionship he'd felt with the first woman who didn't try to fake that she understood baseball, but was willing to learn. He didn't really know what the hell it was, but he felt like telling her exactly what he was thinking. "It's too bad we had to meet under such bizarre circumstances."

"Why's that?" She looked up again, her lips parting slightly, her ridiculous but adorable cowboy hat casting a shadow over her delicate cheeks. "Because you think you could have made a baseball fan out of me?"

He froze in his spot, the desire to kiss her hitting him as hard as that line drive he just missed. "Yeah," he said, taking off her hat so he could get closer. "And I could, too."

Face to face, as though it were the most natural thing in the world, he curled his arms around her waist and she did the same around his neck. Their heights were damn near perfect, he thought. Her eyes at his mouth, just a simple head tilt apart.

"You're going to sign the paper, aren't you?"

He nodded once. With her gazing up at him with that engaging look of gratitude on her face, he just had to dip his head about three inches…open his mouth to meet hers and…

He kissed her.

She tasted like salt and beer and mint. Her lips were warm and soft and when they opened to him, he skimmed the delicate inside flesh of her mouth with his tongue. His head buzzed with the instant pleasure, and he tensed his arms around her, angling his head to make the kiss more intense and longer.

And it lasted just long enough to start a fire in his body.

Slowly she pulled away. Her eyes were closed, but that beautiful mouth formed a smile. For some reason, that pleased him more than anything. She hadn't yanked away and called him a jerk who'd forgotten the serious reason she'd come to him. She looked like she thoroughly enjoyed being kissed by him.

"I'll tell you what," she whispered, her mouth still close enough to almost feel the movements of her lips.

"What?"

"I'll teach Callie baseball and I'll even buy her a Yankee baseball cap. Okay?"

A million clashing emotions rushed through him, but he tamped them all down.

"You do that, sweetheart." He slid his hands over the curves of her waist and up the sleek, tight muscles of her back.

Then she lifted her face toward him again, a victorious light in her magical eyes. "You have no idea how happy you've made me."

This time she leaned into him and initiated the kiss, all that happiness translating into an instant connection between their mouths.

He slanted his head to taste more of her, cupping her face between his hands and then tunneling his fingers into her magnificent hair. He felt himself stir into hardness against her stomach, the flare of desire shooting through his veins like liquid lightning.

He had to get control or she would most definitely miss her flight. Pulling away, he stroked her lower lip with the tip of his finger, resisting the urge to slide that finger into her mouth, where his tongue had been.

"Nothing like a little baseball to warm a lady up," he said with a smile.

She just smiled and pulled farther away, not contradicting him on the reason for her sudden light and lusty mood. She'd won her game, and they both knew that accounted for her surprising display of affection.

"Come on, sweetheart." He tugged her toward the cab stand he knew was around the corner of the stadium. "Let's get to the airport."

As they reached the stand, he opened the door of the first available waiting cab. "After you."

But she didn't move. "No, Cam, you don't have to go all the way to the airport. Just—" she glanced at his pocket "—sign." She gave him a heartbreaking look. Half pleading. Half regretful. "Just sign the paper and I'll be on my way."

"And miss making out with you in the cab? Are you crazy?"

She let out a quick laugh. "I think we've made out enough for one night."

She reached toward his jacket pocket, but he backed away. "Then we'll talk."

There went that pretty eyebrow, straight into a disbelieving arch.

He inched her into the cab. "Really," he assured her, unable to resist checking out the backside of the body he'd been holding. "We'll talk."

Not that he'd mind kissing her in the back of a cab for an hour, but it was time to talk.

Kissing Cameron McGrath had been stupid. And incredible.

Okay, it had been incredibly stupid.

But Jo had been so pleased that he'd agreed to sign

the paper, and so...turned on by him. She'd *wanted* to kiss him. And, truth be told, she wanted to kiss him again.

But she shimmied to the far side of the cab, and he left a good foot of seat between them. Maybe he did want to *talk*.

If he would just sign the damn consent form, she'd kiss him silly from here to Kennedy. God, it had been so long since any man turned her on like this. She'd been gun-shy for years after her marriage debacle, which had only been an ugly confirmation that her mother's theory about men was absolutely right: they *leave*.

She'd kept herself too busy fixing wrecks to pay much attention to the men who came through the door of her shop. One, maybe two had caught her eye and she'd had the occasional interlude with them, but she couldn't remember anyone who made her legs turn watery and put that twinge in her tummy.

Katie, on the other hand, had pretty much been addicted to that twinge and not only had her legs turned to water, but her brain basically disintegrated in the company of a sexy guy, too. Now, that led to some big messes, and fixing those wrecks had sucked up the rest of Jo's personal time.

"So, where's the father?"

His question surprised her—almost like he'd been following her train of thought. "You mean...Callie's father?" She hated to say the baby's name. She didn't want him to form the least bit of an interest in knowing her. In meeting her. If he did, he'd fall in love, of course. Everyone fell in love with Callie on first sight. She was a replica of Katie, gorgeous, beguiling and downright irresistible.

"Were they married?" he asked.

She sniffed. "He was."

"Oh." There was a definite note of disappointment in his voice.

She gave him a tight smile. "In her defense, she didn't know—at first."

"And he doesn't want to take care of his own kid?" Disappointment turned to disgust.

"He'd rather his wife and kids didn't know about Callie. He gave up parental rights long before the baby was born."

Cameron blew out a breath and looked out his window. "Why the hell did she mess around with a married man? Was she stupid or something?"

"No," Jo said quickly. "She was very smart. Brilliant about some things. The business, the books. All that stuff. But…she had a weakness for smooth-talking, good-looking guys. And they, most of the time, had a weakness for her."

He snorted softly. "You know what they say about the apple and the tree."

Jo's spine stiffened at the comment, and she turned to him, stabbing a single finger in his direction. "Look, you can throw your insults at Katie. After all, she's your little sister and she was a royal pain in the butt. But you cannot—I repeat, *cannot*—insult Aunt Chris. That woman was a saint."

"*Aunt* Chris, is it?" This time he choked a bitter laugh. "We are definitely not talking about the same Christine McGrath."

Could she be hearing him right? He *did* blame Chris.

"Why was she a pain in the butt?" he asked before she could set the record straight. At her questioning look, he clarified, "Katie. You said she was a pain in the butt."

"She was…" How could she put it? "A poor judge

of character." Because Katie longed for a man to fill the void that having no father had caused.

A spurt of guilt accompanied that thought. God, she didn't want that to happen to Callie. But it hadn't happened to Jo—and she'd been raised without a father. That desperation didn't *have* to happen to a fatherless girl.

"Was she a—" He gave her a meaningful look, and she gave him a point for avoiding the ugly word.

"No," Jo assured him. "She had morals. She wasn't a loose girl. She just got involved with a married man and got pregnant. Not the first girl in history to make that mistake."

"Were you close to her?"

"Like sisters."

In the shadows of the cab, she thought she saw him wince at that. "How'd you meet her?"

"Chris came to Sierra Springs when I was three, almost four. She was pregnant and looking for work. Evidently, she and my mom—the only other single mother in town at the time—hit it off. Mom gave her a job at her beauty salon and they practically lived next door to each other. Chris was like my aunt, which is what I've always called her. And Katie was just always…there. Ever since I can remember."

For a long time he didn't say anything. He stared out her window, his expression pained. Jo studied his face, the heart-stopping features changing from dark to light with the passing cars. His deep-blue eyes had a faraway look, his square jaw clenched with some unspoken emotion.

Don't think too much, Cam. Don't change your mind. Just sign the damn petition.

She didn't want to push too hard, but her nerves felt frayed from waiting. "Have we talked enough yet?" She sucked in a quiet breath, and held it while she waited for his answer.

His gaze shifted from the world outside to focus on her, the hint of seduction back in his eyes as his expression relaxed. "Ready to make out?"

She almost laughed at the tease. "Will you sign that paper now?"

His lips curled up in a smile, and he moved imperceptibly closer, his now-familiar scent tickling her nose as he invaded the little bit of space between them. "You are persistent, I'll give you that."

"You should see me rough out a dent."

"I'd like to," he whispered, closing more space.

She tapped his rock-hard chest. "Sign."

He slid his hand under her hair. "Kiss."

"That's blackmail."

"Actually, it's extortion." He moved so close she could see the dilated pupils against his irises, even in the unlit cab.

She forced herself to turn to the window, in time to read a green-and-white highway sign as they passed it. "We're almost at the airport."

His gaze dropped over her face, settling on her mouth. She had to fight the urge to pull his head closer, to press her mouth against his again. Instead, she reached into his suit jacket pocket and closed her fingers around the envelope.

He must have known what she was doing, but he didn't stop her.

"Here." She held it out to him. "Do you need a pen?"

He didn't take the paper, instead he dropped back against the seat with an air of defeat. "I need to read it."

Her heart sank. "It's long. A lot of legalese."

"My native tongue."

The cabbie suddenly knocked on the privacy window. "What airline?"

Oh, Lord. They'd arrived at JFK and she still didn't have his signature.

She opened the envelope while Cameron leaned forward to talk to the cab driver. The document was short, just two pages. On the bottom of the second page was a line for his signature. Digging through her bag, she found a ballpoint pen.

"Here." She handed both to him.

He just shook his head. "Inside. I'll read it in the terminal."

She had to accept that.

The cab pulled to a stop at the departures terminal. While Cameron paid for the cab, she climbed out, holding the paper.

"You don't have any other bags?" he asked as they headed into the terminal.

"I didn't plan on staying."

He shook his head. "What if I didn't sign that paper? Were you going to just go home?"

"I didn't come to New York to sightsee," she told him as they stepped into the light. She tapped his chest with the edge of the folded document and slapped the pen into one of his hands. "Here. You read it and I'll check in."

She turned from him, leaving him with his legalese, her heart thudding with each step. Please sign. Please sign.

Under the massive display board of flight times and gates, she imagined the words he was reading. It was simple enough. All it said, in a series of endless sentences, was that he, as the oldest sibling and closest living blood relative, released all rights and duties to Callie Katherine McGrath.

Suddenly she felt him behind her, a warm, strong

presence. He placed two hands on her shoulders and gently squeezed. "No can do, sweetheart."

She spun around. "What?"

"Besides the fact that there's no proof this Callie Katherine McGrath is related to me, this document requires notarization."

"No, it doesn't. I already checked that before I left California."

He pointed to a string of minuscule words across the bottom of the page. "New York is one of the states this line refers to."

"I have the proof in my purse," she insisted, but the definitive shake of his head caused the blood to drain from hers. "Can we find a notary?"

"At ten-thirty at night?"

Disappointment made her dizzy and she swore under her breath. If he had too much time, he could change his mind. He had every right, she knew, but she'd hoped this would be a ten-minute conversation.

"There's nothing we can do tonight," he said softly. "In the morning we'll go to my office, get it notarized and you can catch a later flight."

"But…but…"

"Come on," he said, putting his arm around her and leaning a little too close. "You can darken my doorstep, after all."

Cam grinned and reached out to keep Jo's hat on her head. The rim threatened to tip backward as she gazed up at the top floor of his fifty-two-story building. When she did, the ends of her hair grazed her backside, an image he found wickedly arousing.

"You *live* here?"

He laughed softly. "Don't sound so shocked. It's the

Upper East Side. People kill for an apartment in this building."

"But it's a skyscraper, not a home."

"Don't tell me you're afraid of heights?"

She gave him an incredulous look. "I climb mountains."

"You do?"

"Did Shasta and Whitney in the same year," she said, her gaze sliding up the building again. "So I suppose I can do your monolith."

"Fortunately we have elevators for the faint of heart."

Inside the building, he greeted Gervaise, who nodded to Jo, seemingly unfazed that Cam was bringing home a strange woman in a cowboy hat and boots. Not that his showing up with an unfamiliar woman would surprise his doorman. But the rodeo gear might have elicited at least a raised eyebrow.

"I'm on the thirty-second floor," he told Jo as they entered the chrome-and-mirrored elevator. "Wait'll you see the view."

As the car shot up, she crossed her arms and leaned against the back wall, then closed her eyes.

"Are you okay?" he asked. "This is an express, and some people get a little queasy."

She shook her head and smiled. "I guarantee you this doesn't bother me."

But something did. "You don't have to worry," he said. "I have an extra bedroom."

Her eyes flashed open. "I wasn't worried about that, either."

The elevator stopped at his floor and he pulled his keys from his pants pocket. "You didn't really think I was going to sign that without some kind of judge or notary to officiate, did you?"

Her look confirmed that she had thought exactly that.

"Well, maybe some other guy might have, but I'm a lawyer. And whoever told you a signature you wring out of someone in an airport would hold up in court is giving you lousy advice."

"I'm representing myself," she said softly. "And you said you'd sign it. Right before you kissed me."

He opened the door. "You kissed me."

"First. *You* kissed *me* first."

"Well, someone had to take the initiative to get what we both wanted."

She stood outside the door as if the heels of her boots were glued to the hallway carpet. "I *wanted* your signature."

Was that why she'd kissed him? He put his hand on her back and ushered her into the entryway. "Moot point now. Let's not argue in the hall."

She took one step into the apartment, but it looked like it pained her to do so. "I really thought," her voice cracked a little, then she cleared her throat, "I really thought you were going to sign that petition."

"I will." He moved around the living room, turning on a few of his nicest mood-setting lamps, then pressed the button that opened the drapes that covered one entire glass wall. "I bet you don't have views like this in Sierra Springs."

She crossed the room, her eyes trained on the show-stopping vista of lights and water. "Our views are different."

"We're facing east," he explained. "That's the East River, way down there is the Brooklyn Bridge, the—"

She suddenly spun around, sparks shooting from her coppery eyes. "Do you promise?"

He knew what she meant, of course. And he had no

reason to torture her by threatening not to sign. She'd answered any questions he had; he simply wasn't interested in finding out any more gory details about the "saint" who was his mother. He'd sign her paper, but they'd do it legally.

And he had something else to do first. He had to call his brothers, but he knew damn well if he revealed that, she'd start spitting nails. And he didn't want her spitting nails. He much preferred her happy. The way she'd been outside the Stadium. Warm. Affectionate. *Happy.*

"Do you promise, Cam?" she asked again.

But he wouldn't lie. Not even for another one of those temperature-raising kisses. "I'll do the right thing," he said vaguely. "I always do."

"Then we have that in common," she said, finally looking as though she might relax. "That's why I'm here."

She dropped her hat on the sofa, and once again the vision of her on his spare, high-end furniture seemed incongruous. She didn't belong in this Manhattan highrise. Not that she looked uncomfortable, just out of place.

"Feel free to kick off those boots, too, sweetheart." He walked toward the kitchen. "Want a beer?"

"Just water," she said, ignoring his probably not-so-subtle suggestion to start undressing. Instead he saw her wander back to the window.

When he returned to the living room, she was turned toward the view, but speaking quietly on a cell phone.

"Just don't give her that soy stuff again, Mom. She hated it."

Baby talk. It was of no interest to him. From behind, he studied her lazily. Her hair was not as neat as when he'd first seen her, but it tumbled over her back, long and straight and way too tempting to any mortal man.

"'Kay. See you tomorrow." She clicked off and

turned to him, taking the glass of ice-water he held out. "Thank you. I have a nice view, too," she added, clearly sidestepping the unasked question of who she'd called. "No lights at night, though. Just the moon."

He sat on the sofa, hoping she'd join him. "No lights? Where do you live?"

"In the foothills. In an old house that I'm refurbishing."

"Let me venture a wild guess here. You're doing it yourself."

She grinned and dropped into the club chair across from him. "Damn straight. I just finished the kitchen."

He laughed softly and took a swig of beer. "I don't think I've ever met a girl who played with motors, climbed rocks and laid her own tile."

"You still haven't. I don't touch the engines, I do body work. I don't climb *rocks,* I climb *mountains.* And I didn't lay any tile. But I built new cabinets and installed butcher-block countertops." She reached down and slid off her boots with two smooth movements, then planted two little socked feet on the glass coffee table as though it were an ottoman instead of a work of art. "And I defy you to find a single seam in the whole kitchen."

He couldn't help laughing. "A regular Jill-of-all-trades."

"I've been called worse."

"Really?" He could only imagine. "Like what?"

"Tomboy, mostly."

He shook his head and took the excuse to openly regard her from top to bottom. Not voluptuous, certainly. But nothing anyone would ever mistake for a *boy.* "Another wild guess—no one's called you that in, oh, fifteen years."

She rolled her eyes with a sarcastic little exhale, then

let her head fall back on the chair. "Oh, let's see…when was the earthquake? Three months ago. I don't know for a fact, but Katie probably slung that term around three or four times a day. So, yeah, more recently than fifteen years."

It wasn't the first time he'd picked up a hint of rivalry, even something akin to jealousy, when Jo talked about this woman, this supposed sister of his.

"Was that what made her a royal pain in the butt?"

"Among other things." She smiled, her eyes still closed. She surely didn't realize what a sight she made, the narrow column of her neck exposed, her arms wide open, giving him a direct view of the vee in her collar and the hint of cleavage underneath it.

"Such as?"

"Trouble just follows some people around, you know?" She lifted her head and looked at him. "Like that Li'l Abner cartoon character who had the thunder-cloud over his head all the time. You remember that?"

"Vaguely."

She shrugged. "Well, that was our Lady Katie. One gorgeous, wild, irreverent, fearless little pack of problems."

"I got a brother like that," Cam said with a laugh. "The rebel, Colin."

"They could be twins."

Something twisted in his heart. "What do you mean?"

"When I was…looking for information on your family, I found a picture of Colin in an article in *Newsweek*."

He remembered the feature story on Colin's avant-garde architectural design of an opera house in Oregon. "And he looked…like…her?"

She nodded. "The dark hair and eyes. Same face. Only Katie was tiny. Colin looked kind of tall, like you. But they could have been twins."

Until that very moment he hadn't bought the story. Not completely. Part of him had been playing a game, so intrigued by his unexpected guest that he hadn't bothered to take a stand and demand proof of her outrageous claims. He hadn't even really believed her paperwork to be legitimate until he saw it.

Had he really had a sister? Or even a half sister?

And, good God, did he have a niece?

It's up to you, Cam McGrath. You're the oldest. You'll heal the hurt.

He tunneled his hair with his fingers, then ran his hands over his late-day stubble. Oh, man. Was Gram McGrath right?

"Do you have a picture?" he finally asked.

Wordlessly she stood and walked to the entryway where she'd dropped her bag. "I have pictures of Katie and Aunt—"

"Just Katie." He had no interest in seeing his mother.

She pivoted on her stockinged foot. "You better pound out that great big chip on your shoulder, Cam. She wasn't the Wicked Witch of the West."

He rolled his eyes. "Well, she sure as hell wasn't the patron saint of lost children."

"Cameron!" She barked his name so hard he thought she might have stamped her foot at the same time, the color rising in her cheeks. "Would you even consider the fact that maybe you don't know what happened? Has your father told you everything?"

"He told us enough."

"Then why would you hate a woman who was turned away by her husband for being pregnant with *his* child?"

That age-old white light of anger popped in his head, and Cam reached down to his most controlling depths to dim it. He closed his eyes and dropped his head back. "No, sorry, sweetheart. If she was pregnant, it wasn't my dad's baby. She wasn't turned away by anyone. She waltzed out the door to *find herself.*" He put air quotes around the phrase that had always disgusted him, then let his hands fall to his sides, resisting the urge to curse mightily. He *hated* this subject.

Her purse hit his stomach with a thwack, and his eyes popped open at the impact. "Hey!" He choked out the word.

"Well I see mule-headed ignorance is as hereditary as good cheekbones in your family." She stood in front of him, hands on narrow hips, fire in her coppery eyes. "You'll find some letters in there. From your mother to your father. Note that he never read a single one, but had them returned to her."

He narrowed his eyes at her, but a response utterly eluded him. Was it *possible?*

"I think those letters will change your mind about your mother."

He doubted it. "Why do you care about changing my mind? It doesn't help your cause."

She shook her head in bewilderment. "My cause has nothing to do with Christine McGrath. Katie was the mother of the child I want, and she was the idiot who never drew up a will in case something happened to her. But Aunt Chris had a heart of gold, and years ago, someone broke it into a million pieces." She stabbed a single finger toward his face. "She deserves to be remembered by her sons. And loved for the sacrifice she made. Your hatred is misplaced."

He just stared at her, processing the speech. Broken heart? Sacrifice?

He hoisted the bag from his lap and dumped it on the

floor. "Let's just leave my mother out of this. I'll handle the legalities of *your friend's* baby in the morning."

He saw her shoulders sag a little, like some air seeped out of her. "Fine. That's fine." She looked around the room. "Where's that extra bedroom?"

He gestured down a hallway off the dining area. "Last door on your right. There's a bathroom in there, too." He glanced at the bag as though it contained a bomb. "Don't you want that? Don't you need something to sleep in?"

For a moment she just looked at her satchel, then she reached down and unzipped it, pulling out a small, striped cosmetic bag. "I need my toothbrush." She stuck her other hand inside, her gaze still on him as she rooted around, then flipped out something white. "And clean underwear."

She turned on her heel and headed down the hall. "I sleep naked. Everything else in there is for you."

He watched her until she disappeared inside the last door, then dropped his head back with a soft groan. Why would his father lie to them?

After a minute he stared down at the bag, imagining just what contents she'd *brought for him*. His fingers itched to dig through it. To read those letters. To know the truth.

Or at least someone else's version of the truth.

He slowly reached down and pulled out a thick stack of papers, folded and wrapped in a rubber band. Like a dealer cutting the deck, he took one from the middle of the pack and slid one piece of paper out, then unfolded it.

Dear James,
Your daughter has turned four.

He closed it again.
He really didn't want to deal with this. He wanted to

think about anything but the possibility that his father had lied to them. He'd much rather think about the woman who slept *naked,* who was probably in the act of undressing right now in his guest bedroom. But he pulled out another letter at random, his gaze sliding down to the middle of the handwritten page.

> *I long for news, a word, a picture. Anything about my boys. Is Colin riding a bike yet? Does Quinn still climb trees? Is Cam playing baseball this year?*

His heart spiraled straight into his stomach and hit bottom like a boulder.

Oh, man. This changed everything.

Four

The sheets must have cost five hundred dollars. In a guest room, no less. Jo slid her bare legs over the icy-cold cotton—six-hundred thread count if it was one—and punched the down pillow again. Cameron McGrath certainly had the *means* to take care of Callie, if not the motivation.

She reached over to the nightstand and picked up her watch, angling it into the moonlight that peeked in through the blinds.

Ten-thirty, according to the watch she'd stubbornly left on California time. No wonder she wasn't sleepy. She'd timed this trip so she could sleep on the plane. But instead of flying thirty thousand feet over the Midwest right now, she was in a million-dollar Upper East Side apartment, slithering around on Buckingham Palace-quality sheets.

In a different time zone, trying to fix a different kind of wreck. And this boy wasn't just wrecked. He was *totaled*.

Why couldn't she leave well enough alone? How that man handled the memory of his long-lost mother was really none of her business. All that mattered was that he relinquished any rights over his niece so they could each go on their merry way with life.

She'd been so close. Why did she have to slam that final hammer stroke and force him to deal with something he'd obviously buried years ago? He needed a shrink. Not a collision repair expert.

She sucked in a little breath at a sound. Footsteps in the hall. He was still up. At the tap on her door, she pulled the covers higher. Didn't he believe her? She had nothing on under these sheets.

"Jo, are you awake?"

"Just a second." She grabbed the shirt she'd left folded on the nightstand and slipped into it, pinching one snap over her chest before she scurried back under the covers. "Come on in."

A narrow band of light from the hall illuminated him. He'd changed from his suit and wore some kind of baggy pants and a T-shirt. He looked even broader, more masculine than in his business attire. "What's the matter?" she asked.

"I could use some company." His voice sounded like eighty-grit sandpaper, the sound piercing her heart.

She patted the side of the bed. "As long as you stay on top of the covers and on your own side."

He closed the door behind him, cloaking the room in darkness again. She could sense him approaching the bed, smell his scent, feel his warmth. The king-sized mattress dipped with his weight, but he remained on his side.

"I read them," he said simply.

"Good."

"I'll have to tell my brothers tomorrow."

Anxiety trickled through her. Could they step in and stop the adoption? "Of course," she said.

For a long time he said nothing, breathing steadily. As her eyes adjusted, she could make out his form, leaning against the headboard, an elbow propped on his bent leg, a hand behind his neck.

"Now do you want to talk about her?" she finally asked, turning on her side to watch him in the shadows.

He let out a long, slow exhale. "I think I know enough."

That much was probably true. Aunt Chris had written faithfully to her ex-husband, several times a year in the beginning, then on birthdays...and their anniversary. She'd never given up.

"How did you get those letters?" he asked.

"After the earthquake, my mom went to the site of the collapsed apartment complex and pleaded with the demolition company to allow us to go through the personal belongings that had been retrieved. Lots of families did that, but it was harder for us, because we weren't really family. Anyway, my mom knew about Aunt Chris's secret, of course. I didn't. I couldn't figure out why she was so determined to dig through the rubble."

She paused for a moment, remembering the day they'd gone to the site, the pain of picking up fragments of people's lives still vivid and fresh.

"My mom knew there was a strong box where Aunt Chris kept the letters. She found it. I didn't even notice her picking it up. I found something else." She swallowed as she remembered the sad moment of seeing Katie's hat trapped under a bookcase.

"Anyway, she didn't tell me right away. Not until a few weeks ago, when it looked like the adoption would go through uncontested. Then she sprang it on me and I searched you out."

"Did Katie know?"

"About you and your family? No. But the sad part was Aunt Chris was about to tell her." Jo closed her eyes, remembering how her own mother had cried when she'd told Jo the story. "Last March, just before the earthquake, Aunt Chris went back east. She said it was to see some friends, but my mom told me she went to her mother's funeral."

"I saw her there."

Shivers danced up her spine. "What?"

"We had a private ceremony. Just my brothers and Nicole, Quinn's wife, and Grace, Colin's fiancée. It was in Newport, Rhode Island. Outside the gate, I saw a woman watching us. I had this feeling…I thought maybe it was her. We had held off on a ceremony to bury my grandmother's ashes, but since it was part of a groundbreaking for a new building, the date was publicized. She could have found out about it."

The possibility that they'd come so close to a reunion made Jo ache. "When she came back, she told my mother that she'd decided to tell Katie the whole story. She never said what changed her mind."

He grunted in disgust. "What a mess. What a screwed-up mess two people made."

He was right, of course. "But the earthquake hit less than a week later at 6:20 in the morning while they were sound asleep."

"Really? They were asleep? How did Callie survive, then?"

"Miraculously her crib was in an air pocket and the firefighters and rescue workers dug for twenty-four hours to get to her."

"Oh, God." His voice nearly cracked with emotion. "She was the—I saw that on the news. I remember the baby cradled by that firefighter. I remember that."

"And you didn't notice having the same name?" She wished she could see him in the dark, to see his expressions and read the thoughts he didn't share.

"McGrath is a common name. I do remember thinking, though…"

"What did you think?"

"Just what a miracle it was. How that baby lived for a reason."

She couldn't stop the little gasp that escaped her.

"What?" he asked, looking down at her. "What is it?"

"It's just that I think that same thing. That Callie…" She lowered her voice, almost scared to share her revelation with him. "That Callie has a special destiny and if she ends up in some foster home or…or orphanage, she'll never realize it."

He slid down the bed, closer to her. "You really love her." His hand found hers and clasped it.

"Yes, I do. I've loved her since before she was born. I love her and I will do anything to protect her."

He squeezed her hand, then threaded his fingers through hers. "I couldn't want more for her."

Relief washed over her like a shower of warm water. "Thank you." She pulled their locked hands near her heart. "Thank you, Cam."

He eased himself farther down the bed, so that his long, powerful body now lined up with hers, the comforter separating them. Stroking her hair back from her face, he said softly, "Go to sleep now. We have a big day tomorrow."

"Okay. Good night."

He leaned forward and kissed the cheek he'd just caressed. His breath was warm, his lips tender as they touched her skin. When he lifted his head, she turned her face, so their lips lined up. Without a word, he took her mouth in a deep, soulful kiss.

Instant fire shot through her as his tongue took entry, a low moan vibrating from her throat. Oh, it would be so easy. One toss of the covers and she could feel him against her whole body. Her breasts tingled and ached at the mental image of his hands closing over her nipples, his mouth doing the same.

She barely knew him. Wasn't this exactly the kind of risky behavior she had always admonished Katie for?

He dropped some of his weight against her, intensifying the kiss, and she responded by gliding her hands over his arms and back. His muscles were solid, defined, unyielding under the pressure of her hands. He released her mouth but burned her cheeks and throat with more fiery kisses, his hands closing over her shoulders.

The comforter was about to be history.

Slowly he lifted his head, revealing hooded eyes and half-parted lips. He'd managed to hold himself away from her, but she knew that as soon as they gave in to the lust, as soon as they allowed the body contact to happen, she'd feel that he was definitely as aroused as he looked. As she felt.

"Wait," she said softly.

"Wait. Okay," he agreed, none too enthusiastically. "For what?"

She smiled and scooted a bit away. "Oh, I don't know. Maybe until we know each other and have sorted through the legal mess we have between us."

He closed the space she'd made, but still didn't press against her. "The only thing between us is a blanket," he said, his voice still raspy but for an entirely different reason. "And I can *sort through* that in a second."

The idea, and the sexy way he said it, made her whole lower half melt. She fought the need to rock against him. "Look, as good as this feels, it's not right. I told you I do the right thing."

"As do I," he said softly. "So much so that it's a joke with my own brothers."

"So why are you doing this?"

"It feels right."

"It feels *good*. There's a difference."

Slowly he dropped to the bed, his weight next to her but not where they both wanted it—on top of her. "Who's the lawyer here?"

That made her laugh and as she did, he pulled her close to him. The laugh changed into a moan at the demanding hardness of his entire male body and another potent kiss.

"Then, here's my closing argument, sweetheart." He breathed the words into her ear, and every hair on the back of her neck leaped and danced. "I would very much like to make love to you, Jo Ellen Tremaine."

Even the way he said her name inflamed her body. She had to hang on to common sense, because the other five had melted into a pool between her legs.

"You don't want to make love," she told him. "You want comfort. Your heart is heavy, Cam. You're seeking consolation."

"A lawyer *and* a psychiatrist, I see."

She smiled and reached for him, her fingers grazing the rough stubble on his jaw, then nesting into the dark-gold locks of hair. "But not a mechanic."

He laughed and kissed her forehead. "Okay. And you're right."

"About the comfort."

"Yeah." It killed him to admit it, she could tell, but he started to roll away.

For some reason she couldn't stand that. She didn't want him to leave. "If you like, if you can control yourself…" she put her hand on his arm, "you can stay here and sleep next to me. On top of the covers because I really don't have much on underneath."

He let out a tiny grunt under his breath. "I've never had a problem with control. But I can't promise that I won't have X-rated dreams about naked cowgirls working on my…engine."

She gave him a little push. "Don't you listen to me? I don't do engines."

"I couldn't say *body*. It was too obvious."

She laughed softly again. "And what makes you think I'm a cowgirl? Because I wear a hat and boots? Everyone dresses like that where I live." She didn't, usually, but there was no reason to reveal why she'd worn the hat.

"No, not the hat or boots," he said at the same time his hand moved slowly from the collar of her shirt, down the vee neck, pausing at the single fastened snap. "It was these rodeo buttons that gave it away."

Lord above, she knew exactly what was coming next.

Cam felt her whole body tighten in anticipation of his touch. He sucked in a breath, inhaling the warm, womanly fragrance of her in his bed.

He lifted the snap, then let the material fall back on her skin without unfastening it. "Whoever called you a tomboy was blind and brainless."

"She had a brain. She just didn't use it all the time."

He didn't want to talk about Katie anymore. And he sure as hell didn't want to talk or think about his mother tonight. Maybe Jo was right. Maybe he was looking for a consolation prize. And as sweet and sexy and fantastic as this woman felt in his arms, taking his comfort by having sex with her wasn't the right thing to do.

He stilled his anxious fingers and laid his hand on her breastbone. Under his palm, her heart thudded just like his. Her blood raced, just like his. And he'd bet if he went exploring, he'd find her body was fully aroused, just like his.

But she hadn't gotten on a plane and traveled three thousand miles to get laid. She'd taken a huge risk to "do the right thing." She never had to tell the courts or the McGraths about the existence of this baby.

"Go to sleep, sweetheart," he said softly.

"I can't."

"Am I bothering you?"

He could practically feel her smile. "That's one way of putting it."

He moved his hand up to her throat and tucked his fingers in a safe place, along the line of her delicate jaw. He liked holding her like this. Even with the stupid blanket between them. He liked it. And this level of comfort, he'd earned.

"Try to sleep, Jo."

They hardly moved for the next few hours, as he drifted in and out of sleep and braced himself for the onslaught of old enemies that had been known to haunt him on bad nights. Images of a dark-haired woman with a gentle laugh, on her knees in a garden. But none came.

But he did dream of a girl. A beautiful girl with long, auburn hair and her own distinct laugh, also on her knees, but in front of him. Her hands were demanding. Her mouth was accommodating. Her talents were indescribable.

The powerful ache of an erection punched him awake

with a start. And the first thing he saw was a mane of reddish hair splayed over the pillow and the sweet face of Jo Ellen in repose, the golden fingers of dawn slipping through the blinds to light her skin. Leaning up on an elbow, he studied her, unencumbered by the need to figure out what she was thinking, free to just feast his eyes on the "cowgirl mechanic."

Long, thick eyelashes swept the tender skin under her eyes. Her nose was slightly upturned at the end to give her some attitude and, oh, that mouth. Wide and symmetrical, with a little pout to the lower lip. His ache deepened as he remembered the taste of that lip and what it had done to him in his dreams.

The blanket had drifted down, revealing her cotton shirt, the single snap still fastened. But the fabric was pushed back enough for him to see the creamy underside of a small, delicate breast. The need to touch it made his hands hurt and his throat go dry.

Why did this woman get to him? He was no monk, hard up for a quickie. He'd been with Amanda less than three weeks before, and he'd always been able to control his sexual urges as well as he controlled every other aspect of his life. But this woman. This Jo…

She stirred and he waited for those intriguing eyes to open. To give him tacit permission to touch her. To kiss her. To taste her.

His pulse pumped spurts of blood through his body, making him harder and hotter with each passing second. She turned slightly toward him, revealing more of her breast through the opening of her shirt.

He wanted to say something to wake her. Something clever, something cool. But there was nothing cool about the way he felt. Maybe he could just *kiss* her awake.

He placed his fingers on the snap of her blouse.

It clicked open with almost no effort. She didn't move. Slowly, reverently, unable to stop himself, he caressed the skin between her breasts.

She shuddered with a ragged breath as he dipped his head and kissed her mouth. Want and need coiled his body into a knot, a low growl rumbled in his chest. She shifted, offering him her breast, allowing his palm to cover the smooth, silky nipple. Her mouth opened, her tongue immediately seeking his.

She was definitely awake. And definitely giving permission to proceed.

He eased the blanket farther down, anxious to get rid of their covers, their clothes, of anything that came between them.

A flash of reason interrupted his erotic thoughts. *Plenty* came between them. Life and history and families came between them, but when she lifted one long, bare leg out of the covers and wrapped it around his, all those reasonable thoughts evaporated.

"I dreamed about you," he whispered against her lips. "I've been wanting you all night long."

She responded by sliding her hand under his T-shirt, her hot, talented fingers grazing the skin of his stomach and his own hardened nipples.

She nibbled the edge of his jaw, the heat of her mouth and her hands searing his skin. "I couldn't sleep," she whispered. "And I had my own X-rated thoughts."

The idea almost did him in, and he ground his hips against her as though he could thrust himself where he wanted to be. Inside her. Deep, deep inside her. "Tell me."

"No. You." Her voice was husky and sweet at the same time. "A good shrink always analyzes dreams."

He smiled. "You were on your knees."

That earned a quick laugh. "That's generally how I work."

Her hand moved slowly down his chest, back down his belly, and her fingers dipped into the waistband of the sleep pants he wore. He lifted his body to give her access, and when he did, their gazes met.

He smiled at her sleepy, sexy, hungry expression. "You're beautiful, you know that?"

She stunned him by shaking her head a little. "You're dying for sex. You'd say anything right now."

"No." He lifted himself away from her, as though that controlled action could prove her wrong. "That's not true."

"You're not dying for sex?"

"I'm...*interested,* yes."

She responded with a soft sigh. A hint of resignation and excitement mixed her eyes. "Me, too." Her fingertip almost grazed the tip of him. Fire shot through his groin and he squeezed his eyes shut to keep from thrusting himself into her hand.

"Good," he managed to say. "But are you trying to tell me you don't know you're beautiful?"

She didn't respond, her fingers poised dangerously close to a switch he didn't want her to throw.

Slowly he reached down and encircled her wrist, easing her hand away from him, then lowered himself on her. Still a dangerous place, with his erection slamming somewhere in the vicinity of her lower half, the blanket providing woefully little separation, but he had more control than when her hand was in his pants.

"Listen to me, Jo Ellen."

"You have my undivided attention," she said wryly with a soft rock of her hips.

"I think you're a beautiful woman. All beautiful and all woman." He added a thrust of his own for emphasis.

And pleasure. "And if you want to, only if you want to, I can give you mindless, senseless, endless satisfaction. But not because I'm dying for it." He bent closer and kissed her, nibbling on that fantastic lower lip before releasing her. "And not because I need comfort." He slid his hand up to that sweet breast again, grazing the nipple with his thumb. "And not because you need to thank me for some perceived good deed."

Her eyes flashed as she jerked out from underneath him. "You had me right up until that last one."

The loss of her stunned him almost as much as her sudden turnabout. He searched her face for an explanation. Was she mad? Insulted? "What do you mean?"

In one smooth move she was away from him, the covers safely pulled over her. "I'm not going to sleep with you to get you to sign that consent petition."

"I know that," he insisted. "I just…I just want you to know my motives were…" Good God, he sounded like a teenager begging for sex. Forget *that*.

In an instant he was up and off the bed. "You're right. This—" he made a gesture indicating the two of them "—is loaded with too many issues."

She shimmied up, holding the covers over her chest. "And you don't *do* issues, do you, Cameron?"

"Do me a favor, Jo, and spare me the pop psychology and stick to fixing dented cars."

As soon as he said it, he regretted it. The pretty flush of pleasure drained from her cheeks, leaving pale, pained alabaster skin in its wake.

"Sorry," he said quickly, shaking his head as though he could erase the words. "I didn't mean that as harshly as it sounded."

"No need to apologize." Her voice was as flat as the look in her eyes. "I was thinking the same thing last night."

All her spark disappeared. Man, he sure doused that fire with record speed.

"Could I take a shower now?" she asked.

And wash the remnants of him off, she might as well have added. Swallowing a curse aimed only at himself, he nodded toward the bathroom. "Make yourself at home. I have a few calls to make, then we'll get going."

He turned and walked down the hall without closing the bedroom door. In the living room, he saw the evidence of last night's hours of self-discovery. A pile of handwritten letters, Jo's open bag, her boots, her cowboy hat.

He picked up the hat and ran his finger over the satin band inside, feeling the bumps of a monogram. He turned it over and read the gold letters embroidered on the inside.

"Lady Katie."

Dropping the hat on the sofa as if it had burned him, he went into his office to call Quinn.

Five

"**S**he was *what?*"

"When she left home, she was pregnant," Cam calmly repeated into the phone, imagining Quinn's dark eyes flashing with the same disbelief he'd felt the night before. He'd gotten most of the story out, after Quinn stopped joking long enough to take him seriously. He'd described Jo's auspicious arrival, the letters and the fact that their mother and sister had been killed in an earthquake.

"That's why she left." But the story got more complicated, and Quinn wasn't going to like it any more than he did. "Evidently Dad didn't believe the baby could be his because he'd had a vasectomy after Colin was born."

His brother was quiet for a moment, and through the phone Cam could hear the clanging of hammers and whine of buzzsaws, and pictured Quinn in the midst of the beachfront resort he was restoring with his wife.

"This Jo character sounds like a real wacko, bro," Quinn said dismissively. "Better send her back to La-La Land. Hey, I know it's a few months from now, but we're looking at arrival dates for Colin's wedding. When are you going up to Newport?"

Denial. He recognized it from a thousand miles away. "Listen to me. I read about twenty letters our mother wrote to Dad. Letters, evidently, he wouldn't even read. Quinn, she wasn't lying. That much I knew by one in the morning. Vasectomies aren't foolproof, but apparently her history worked against her and he made her leave."

"Her *history?* She was a *tramp,* Cam. She ran away from home at seventeen and ran away from Dad at thirty-something. Anyway, she's dead. And so's this alleged daughter." Quinn paused for a second, then his tone turned casual. "Nic wants to get to the wedding a few days early."

"The daughter had a baby," Cam said quietly, refusing to let his brother derail this conversation. "We have a niece who survived an earthquake and she's alive and up for adoption."

Quinn copped a dramatic voice. "Stay tuned for the next episode of *Days of Our Lives.*"

He knew Quinn would joke. That's how he handled anything uncomfortable. Colin, on the other hand, rebelled against society. And Cam? Well, he just controlled everything he possibly could—including anything vaguely resembling an emotion.

"This is serious, man. Dad must have threatened her that if she didn't have an abortion—"

He heard Quinn's sharp intake of breath and recognized the stab of pain that he'd felt the night before, but continued quickly with the story. "He swore he'd never love the child and would turn us against it, and against…Mom." The word sounded foreign on his lips.

"An abortion?" Quinn's voice had lost all humor. "Have you talked to him yet?"

"No. I wanted to talk to you and Colin first and give Colin the option of having that discussion, since it should be done in person."

"Jeez," Quinn said softly. "What a helluva mess."

"No kidding. Jo really wants to adopt the baby." He glanced toward the empty hallway, expecting her to emerge from the guest bedroom any minute. "I have to sign some papers that say we won't ever try to seek custody. I'm going to—"

"Whoa, just a second, buddy boy. Sign? Are you out of your mind? She could be a total scam artist or a flake."

Cam swiveled away from the door, catching the rays of morning sunlight streaking across the New York skyline. "She's not a flake," he said in a purposely soft voice. He closed his eyes to block the million-dollar view, instead visualizing Jo's face just before he'd kissed her. "She's not a scam artist, either. She's kind of…" How could he describe the cowgirl mechanic? "She's extraordinary, actually."

Quinn groaned softly. "Extraordinary in bed?"

Cam hesitated a second too long.

"You *slept* with her?" Quinn nearly choked.

"No, I didn't." He couldn't help but smile. "Not yet, anyway."

Quinn snorted. "Think with the right body part, man. Maybe this woman's Aunt Christine *was* our mother. But you don't have any proof that her daughter was Dad's. Now this nutcase shows up and wants you to sign some papers. And next, you watch, she'll want money."

"I saw pictures of…Katie. She could be Colin's twin sister," he countered. "Or even yours. And—" the image in his mind shifted to his mother's slanted handwriting "—I've seen the evidence. Trust me and my lawyer's gut, okay? This is the real deal."

Quinn was a gut-driven man himself, confirmed by the soft curse he mumbled as a few seconds ticked by. "Have you talked to Colin?" he finally asked.

"Not yet. You know how he gets." Worked up. "He's so happy right now. I just thought I'd tell you first."

"Hey, I'm happy, too," Quinn countered. "Didn't stop you from screwing up my day."

Cam laughed a little. "Listen, Jo is not a fruitcake. Not a wacko. I'm sure she'll be a great—"

"Wait, Cam. Wait a second." Quinn paused and sighed low and long. "Maybe this baby belongs in our family."

The sudden turnabout, stated with such underlying conviction, stopped Cam cold. "Well, you could make that argument, yeah, but I don't want a kid and neither do you."

"Well, I *better* want one."

The implication was obvious. And astounding. "What?" It was Cam's turn for disbelief. "Is Nic pregnant?"

"Either that or I make her throw up every morning," he said with a laugh. "Always a possibility."

A mess of responses collided in Cam, and he seized the most comfortable one. "That's great news. Congratulations, bro."

"Thanks. We're pretty excited. We were going to tell everyone at Colin's wedding. She's only a few weeks pregnant, so we'll be past the three-month mark then."

"Is everything okay? Nic's feeling good?"

"Oh, yeah. Just tired, hungry." He could almost hear Quinn beam with pride across the miles. "And flat-out gorgeous."

Cam smiled into his phone. "That's great, man. Really. I won't mention it to Colin when I call him, if you want to pop the big surprise yourself."

"You're definitely letting him in on this, too?"

"I can't sign this agreement without talking to both of you and Dad, too. You'd have a right to adopt her, too, you know. Of course, you have your hands full now, and Jo, she really loves this kid like family."

"*Like* family isn't family." There was that serious tone again. It sounded out of character from Quinn. Must be the pregnancy hormones in the air down in Florida.

"What are you getting at, Quinn?"

"Maybe we owe this child a family, a name, a home."

A cool chill blew over Cam. He'd had that same thought, late last night, reading those letters that told about a girl named Katie who must have had quite a personality. He'd felt a brotherly pride, but hadn't been able to articulate what Quinn just did.

"She's in California, Quinn. Being raised by someone who loves her. We don't have any right—"

"We have every right to find out if she's really related to us and, if she is, what kind of home she'll be in."

He heard a noise behind him and spun the chair around to see Jo standing in the doorway of his office, her arms crossed, wet strands of hair darkening the fabric of her shirt. How long had she been eavesdropping?

"You gotta trust me, Quinn," he said, his gaze meeting hers as she entered the room and dropped into the single chair across from his desk.

"I trust you. You're the smartest, coolest guy I know. After me."

Cam resisted the urge to smile, knowing she wouldn't like that reaction. She knew damn well who he was talking to, and what it was about. "So shut up and let me do the right thing."

"Just be sure you know what the right thing is, Cam," Quinn insisted. "Is this Jo character the best person to raise someone in our family? Will she be a good mother? Is her life stable? Does she do drugs? Is she legit?"

Cam realized, with a bit of a shock, that he didn't know much at all about "this Jo character." "She's legit," he responded. "She owns a business." He studied the way she gnawed on that pretty lower lip, her sharp gaze trained on him. How had Quinn described Nicole? Flat-out gorgeous. Well, if that was an attribute for mother-hood, Jo was overqualified.

He winked at her, but she just arched an eyebrow and let every bit of body language show him she had no intention of leaving and no shame about listening.

"Listen," Quinn lowered his voice, probably not wanting to be heard by construction workers. "Just because you don't want a kid doesn't mean Nic and I couldn't handle another one. Or Colin and Grace. Who knows? I mean, if this story is true, then we have a responsibility."

"It's true."

"Well then, you know what Gram McGrath always said about you."

Cam's chest ached as he looked at Jo. Aw, hell. Maybe he didn't want to "heal the hurt." Because if he didn't sign that paper, it would break her heart. "Yeah, I know what she said."

"She was never wrong, bro." Quinn laughed knowingly. "So who's going to California to check out this Jo character's story? You or me?"

He held her questioning gaze, as she toyed with a strand of wet hair and watched him. She looked curious and cool and as alluring in the morning light as she had been in the darkest hours of the night. If anybody was checking out this Jo character, it was Cam.

"I'm on it, bro," he assured Quinn.

"Just don't be on *her* until you know what you're dealing with."

Cam couldn't promise that.

By the time Cameron hung up with his brother, Jo knew the plan was falling apart before her very eyes.

"He wants the baby," she stated simply, leaning back in the chair and taking in the posh surroundings of his home office.

He shook his head. "No, that's not what he said."

"He wants you to take the baby."

"No, no, that's not what we decided, either."

What *we* decided. She loathed the fact that her fate and Callie's fate were in the hands of these controlling, smart, successful men. She was Callie's real aunt, regardless of the bloodlines. But would a judge see it that way? "So what did you two masters of the universe decide?"

He held up a hand as though he could stop the sarcasm that rolled in his direction. "We didn't decide anything."

"It sure sounded like some deciding was going on."

"Didn't your mother teach you it's rude to snoop on other people's conversations?"

She gave him a tight smile. "My mother taught me to fight for what I believe is right. I don't really give a hoot what you two are cooking up. If you won't sign this piece of paper…" she produced the folded document from her back pocket, "then I'll fight you in court and I'll win."

"I don't want it to come to that, Jo."

She threw the paper on his desk. "Then sign."

"It's not just me. I have two brothers."

"And at least one of them is going to have his own baby," she said, giving him a knowing look. "I heard. And the other one's about to get married. And you," she made a sweeping gesture toward the rest of his apartment, "live like the bachelor millionaire who obviously doesn't have room in his life for a baby." She leaned forward, trying to contain the heat of her temper. "So let me have what Katie left to me."

He regarded her intently, his dark blue gaze direct as he no doubt considered his lawyerly response. "Technically she didn't leave this child to you."

Bingo, counselor.

"And technically she didn't leave her to you, either." She stood and pointed to the paper on his desk. "Are you or are you not going to sign that?"

His head shook slowly. "Not yet."

It hit her like a nine-pound hammer, and she bit back a vicious curse in response. Damn him. Damn damn *damn* him. When she thought of how close she almost came to giving him her body that morning, her stomach lurched.

Without a word, she turned on her boot heel and headed for the living room. Her work here was done. Mission failed.

She'd find another way.

She scooped up the letters and pictures from the coffee table and stuffed them into her bag, her hands shakier than she'd like. Throwing the strap over her shoulder, she seized the hat and slammed it on her head.

As she reached the door, he grabbed her elbow just tight enough to bring her to a complete halt. "I'm going with you."

She spun around and almost choked in his face. "No, you are not."

"I want to see your home. And shop. I want to meet my niece and see where—where my mother lived."

That last one almost got her. She had such a soft spot for Aunt Chris, who had loved her as much as she'd loved her own daughter. Sometimes Chris even loved Jo more, when Katie was particularly stubborn and immature.

But that's not why he wanted to go to California. He wanted to take the baby away from her. All he'd have to do is charm one of those Child Services women, and bam! Callie would be his.

Again, her stomach turned at the thought.

He reached toward her, to touch her face, and she jerked her head back. "Don't. Don't." She shook her head just as an ugly thought took shape.

She could still hear the implication in the "guy talk" with his brother.

No, I didn't…. Not yet, anyway.

Was sex a stipulation for his signature? God, she hoped not. She wanted to respect him more than that, wanted to believe she'd been attracted to someone better than that. Because she certainly had been attracted. *Attracted?* She'd been absolutely ready to rock and roll right into ecstasy less than an hour ago.

She purposely narrowed her eyes and lowered her voice. "Would that paper be signed right now if I had slept with you this morning?"

"No. That wouldn't have changed anything."

Tugging the shoulder bag higher, she turned the knob with her free hand. "But we'll never know, will we?"

He slammed a flat hand on the door before she could open it. "You will not leave with that thought in your head."

"Will you quit trying to boss me around?" she retorted. "You can't keep me here. You can't tell me what to think. And you sure as hell can't come with me. God, you're just like Katie. Selfish and manipulative to the core."

"For someone who's hell-bent on raising her child, you sure manage to get a lot of digs in on dearly departed Katie. Did you love her or hate her?"

Her blood nearly boiled over with resentment. "Spare me the pop psychology." She let his earlier bitterness echo in her tone. "Stick to the law, counselor."

He reached up and slowly took her hat off, turning it over to reveal the inside band. "This was her hat, wasn't it?"

"Yes."

"Why do you wear it?"

The resentment melted with the ache of grief. He would never understand how her heart broke when she'd retrieved Katie's hat from the earthquake debris. Or why she'd impulsively grabbed the hat on her way out the door when she'd left for the airport, just to have a piece of the audacious little Katie along for the ride. "I thought it might bring me good luck." She rolled her eyes. "Obviously, I was wrong."

He shook his head and looked hard at the hat. "I don't understand your motives."

She yanked Katie's hat away. "Quit being such a lawyer. My motives are not tough to figure out. There's a little girl in California who has no mother. I love her. I made sure her mother was healthy for nine months. I was in the room when she was born. I have already sacrificed more for her than I would for my own child. It's no crime to want to raise her. I'm not kidnapping her."

"But you are using every trick you know to garner my signature."

Her gaze slid toward the bedroom. "Not every trick."

"That wouldn't have made any difference," he said quietly. "I still wouldn't have signed it."

"Do you know how easily I could have skipped this trip to New York and no one would ever have been the wiser? Callie doesn't ever have to know the truth. I came here because it was *'the right thing to do.'* Period."

"I realize that," he said, finally moving his hand away from the door. "And I respect it."

That gave her some measure of satisfaction. "I have to get home. Callie needs me."

"I'll come down with you to find a cab."

"I can handle it."

He laughed ruefully. "I doubt there's anything you *can't* handle, Jo Ellen. But it would make me feel like a gentleman."

Spinning around, she stabbed a single finger in his chest. "You want to feel like a gentleman? Then sign that paper and let me raise that child without a shadow over her life. I swear I only have the best motives for doing so."

"I can't. Not yet."

She sighed, tired of the fight. This time she yanked the heavy apartment door open. "I'll inform the Child Services people about you next week when I meet with them." She had no idea what would happen after that. "I'm sure they'll contact you."

She stepped into the hall, but he reached out and stopped her with that firm grip again. "Don't leave like this. Give me time to figure out what's the best thing to do, to talk to my brothers. We need to sort out the facts and decide what to do."

She knew what they would do. The three of them would come swooping into Sierra Springs on their proverbial white horses to rescue their baby niece and bring her home to their happy, whole families. They'd cloak themselves in righteousness and family values and pat themselves on the back for being so damn noble.

How could she fight that? "I'll see you in court."

"If not before."

She ignored the thinly veiled threat and walked toward the elevator. Thankfully, he didn't follow.

Six

When Jo pulled the clear protective goggles over her eyes, Callie treated her to a Tinkerbell chime of laughter.

"You like my funny glasses, don'cha, buttercup?"

Callie reached a dimpled hand from her playpen toward Jo's face, then made a happy noise that one of the mountains of child-development books would probably call prespeak or some ridiculous thing.

Jo knew what it was. Baby sounds. Plain and simple. But the books said to encourage talking, so she adjusted the goggles with an expansive gesture.

"Gog-gles," she said slowly. "They protect my eyes while I'm sanding. Which I'm about to do."

Taking a chunky vinyl book from a crowded bookshelf above her desk, Jo handed it to Callie with a smile. "You read this for a few minutes, honey girl. I'll be just on the other side of the glass wall, working that ding out of the Toyota. You'll be able to see me and I'll be able to see you."

Callie frowned and started to chew on the side of the book.

"Or you can eat it, if that's more fun."

Jo bent over and kissed Callie's head, hoping she could finish the rough out quickly. It was a glorious June day and she simply itched to be outside, to take a long hike through the foothills with Callie tucked in her little papoose, breathing the incredible air and figuring out the answers to their messy lives.

"I promise I'll just finish this quarter panel," she told Callie, not bothering to bore the baby with her scheduling problems. The trip to New York two days earlier had thrown her, with the Toyota customer scheduled to show up early the next morning, forcing Jo to work on a Sunday.

On an impulse she flung open the back door that led to the rear parking lot, giving Callie a sliver-size view of the mountains, and allowing warm, fresh air to waft into the shop's back office.

"Just half an hour, angel," Jo promised.

Jo silently blessed the brilliant idea she and Katie had had to redesign their workspaces so Callie could be watched. The glassed-in office ensured that Callie would remain sealed away from the fumes and dust of the body shop. A similar room had been built in the beauty shop next door, but her new tenant had turned it into storage.

When Jo had come to the shop to examine the damage after the earthquake, the tempered glass wall and door in the back of her work bay area had been her biggest concern. But the shop had sustained very little damage. Tools had fallen, and the product shelves in the salon had crashed, but most of the inventory had been plastic.

Not that she had cared, back in those dark days. She remembered the horror and disbelief that consumed everyone, as they focused on the far side of town, several miles out, where the epicenter of the quake had rocked so many buildings to their foundations.

Including the new town-house complex where Katie, Chris and Callie had lived for only six months.

Sliding on a pair of cushy knee pads, a face mask and rubber gloves, Jo dismissed the memory with a silly wave to Callie, who had positioned herself to be able to watch Jo closely. Ever since the earthquake, Callie seemed to hate when Jo left the room, and she watched through the glass like a baby hawk about to be abandoned in the nest. Poor little thing.

Jo waved again, then kneeled at the front end of the minitruck, her tools arranged around her as she considered the paintless dent repair job. She could have this thing hammered out in an hour, tops. Then nothing would keep her from that hike with Callie.

Sticking her head under the front end to get a look at the suspension, she chose a medium-weight hammer. With one light tap to test the give, a familiar vibration danced up her arm.

God, it felt good to have a tool in her hand again. Something she could manage, something she could control. Unlike the whole debacle in New York City, where she'd managed nothing and could barely control her very own body.

She closed her eyes, trying to erase the flashing memory of Cameron McGrath's mouth on hers, of his hand touching her breast. Considering all the things to distract her over the past few days and all the problems she had to face in the next few weeks, the recollection of their brief physical interlude should be the *last* thing on her mind.

But, damn, it was practically the only thing on her mind since she'd gotten on that plane on Friday morning and watched the New York skyline disappear.

And they said men were controlled by hormones. Evidently they weren't the only ones.

She slammed the hammer a little harder and completely inverted the dent. She'd have to forget the hormones, forget the sexual attraction and focus on the problem in front of her.

Her meeting with Child Services was scheduled for Friday, giving her less than a week to come up with a plan, an argument, a rationale, a *something* that would undoubtedly change *nothing*.

Once Mary Beth Borrell learned that Callie had living blood relatives, the social worker would start the paperwork and procedures to contact the McGraths—all of them—and require them to either relinquish consent to Jo or begin adoption proceedings of their own.

Of course, whichever McGrath brother wanted to adopt the baby would be interviewed and deposed, like she had been. Would her baby go to Florida with Quinn and Nicole? Or to Rhode Island with Colin and his fiancée, Grace? Or to New York?

She clobbered the panel with three hard smacks to make up for the spurt of misery that accompanied the thought of losing Callie. She'd been so sure she could shape the outcome of that trip to New York, and at the same time meet her own need to be honest and moral regarding Callie's "family" ties.

Now she was about to be bound and gagged by those very ties.

As she slid out from under the front panel to see the dent inversion, something caught her peripheral vision, a movement in the back office.

The hammer clattered to the floor as the blood rushed out of her head, leaving her dizzy and stunned. A shocked gasp caught in her throat.

She never, *never* expected him so soon.

Cameron McGrath stood next to the playpen, leaning over it and saying something that she couldn't hear through the tempered glass. Then he looked up and their gazes met, sending shockwaves of worry and warmth rolling through her body.

From the playpen, Callie reached up at him like he was her all-time favorite uncle come to shower her with love and presents.

The little traitor.

Without taking off any gear, Jo marched back to the office, whipping the door open with way more force than necessary.

"What are you doing here?" The mask muffled her words and, no doubt, the impact of her demand.

He raked her with one long look, and suddenly she was aware of the boy's T-shirt she wore, the low-slung cargo utility pants, knee pads and clunky work boots. Her hair was pulled up into a sloppy ponytail and she probably had dirt on her face from the undercarriage of the minitruck.

But he just grinned. "This is just how I imagined you looked at work."

Her stomach betrayed her with an unexpected dip. He *imagined* her? She flipped up the goggles and yanked down the mask, moving a few steps to the middle of the room where Callie's playpen sat.

She burned him with what she hoped was a stern look of warning. "How dare you just walk in here."

He pointed over his shoulder to the open door. "Security's pretty lax, if you ask me. You should be more careful."

Damn him and her foolish self for giving him any ammunition against her mothering skills. "We don't have a high kidnapping rate in Sierra Springs," she responded, countering her admittedly weak argument with a sweeping glare over his whole body.

But her gaze got tripped up on the familiar insignia splayed, as it was, over an impressive chest. Yankees, of course. The man was purely pathetic.

He wore faded jeans, just snug enough on narrow hips to scream for closer inspection, but she forced her focus back up to his face and considered that a small victory.

Why couldn't he at least *look* like the monster he was about to become? Did he have to waltz into her shop like some all-powerful golden-haired god?

Callie lost her balance and tumbled down on her diapered bottom, eliciting a quick sound of surprise from Cameron. His whole demeanor changed as he crouched down to Callie's level. "You okay, kid?"

She giggled and clapped merrily, obviously pleased with her ability to snag his attention. She was as flirtatious as her mother—and just as charming.

What good would it do to fight his arrival? He was here and she had to deal with him.

"Prepare yourself, Cam," Jo said as she dragged the goggles through her hair. "You're about to fall in love."

"Ha!" He gave her a brash grin. "That'd be a first."

There went that dumb stomach dip again.

"Yeah?" She crossed her arms and leaned her hip against the desk. "You haven't met Callie McGrath."

Reaching into the playpen, he took her little hand in a pretend handshake. "Pleased to meet you, Miss Callie. I'm Cameron. You can call me Cam. Everyone who likes me does." She curled a fist around his fingers, and he glanced up at Jo. "I believe I even heard Miss Jo Ellen Tremaine say it just now."

Had she called him Cam? "I can't believe you're here already," she admitted, a sigh of defeat coloring her tone. "I haven't even told Child Services about you. I haven't even put together my battle plan."

He laughed a little, releasing his finger, but remaining at Callie's level. "*Battle* plan?"

"This is war. You are going to try and take my baby and I'm going to fight you."

For a long moment, he just stared up at her, then he stood to his full height, surprising her with how tall and substantial a man he was. How could she have forgotten? He'd been on top of her…in bed.

"What makes you think that's why I'm here?"

Her body clutched in expectation as he came around the playpen, toward her. *Expectation?* Did she think he'd come for any reason other than to mess up her life? "Call it a wild guess."

"Well, you're wrong."

The first glimmer of hope since she'd left his apartment started to burn in her heart. "I am? You're not here to try and take her?"

"I had a couple of long talks with Quinn and Colin."

"And?" she asked, forcing herself to breathe.

"And we decided that I should make a trip out here to meet Callie, and see your home and business, to know how—"

"So this is a test? An interview?" She didn't know whether to be insulted or hopeful.

"Just think of it as a…visit. Okay?"

She considered that for a minute, her gaze darting behind him to where Callie had positioned herself in the corner of the playpen. Already the child was mesmerized, her soulful eyes following his every move.

"Are your brothers coming out for a *visit,* as well?" she finally asked.

"Nope. We drew straws." He winked at her. "I won."

A truckload of responses clashed in her head—and heart—as she tried to figure out how to handle this new development. "You know," she told him, "part of me wants to point you to the door and tell you what you can do with your visit."

"And the other part?"

She nodded slowly and levered herself off the desk, taking a step closer to him. "That part says I should welcome this opportunity to show you what a stable and loving home I'm giving Callie."

His gaze dropped over her face, settling on her mouth for a quick second, then back to her eyes. "Who wins? The intelligent, rational, mature Jo or the stubborn, cautious, protective Jo?"

She fought a smile. He was so smart. "They can both be pretty persuasive."

A half smile teased his own lips, and then he reached out and put his hands on her shoulders, his gentle grip forcing her to look up into his face. "So can I. You know I have to do this, and the intelligent, rational, mature Jo accepts that. Right?"

She nodded, and he inched her just close enough to send that thrill of expectation back through her. Speaking of purely pathetic.

Then he dropped a brotherly kiss on the top of her head. "Good girl. I like that part of you."

But what about that other part of her? The achy, craving, lusty Jo who wanted to throw her head back and offer her mouth for a kiss that was *anything* but brotherly.

Well, she'd just have to hammer out that part.

"Let's take a hike."

"A hike?" Did she just tell him to take a hike? Cam sat on the cold cement floor of a body shop and watched Jo sand the last edges of the dent with the finesse of a sculptor crafting a masterpiece.

A *sexy* sculptor. In a damn-near see-through cotton top that was cut off just an inch or two above a slender waist, and work pants that fit so low on her hips that when she leaned under the truck his throat just went dry at what might be exposed. But all he saw was a glimpse of something dark red at the top of her buttocks and hip. Something small. And permanent.

A tattoo.

His whole lower half got heavy at the possibilities.

"Yeah, a hike." She threw him a get-with-the-program look from behind her goggles. "We're in the mountains. That's what we do here on Sunday afternoons. We hike. Or raft the rapids." He could tell she was grinning behind the surgical mask she wore. "Would you rather tackle the whitewater? Or are you too jetlagged from your trip?"

He heard the implied challenge. She might as well have added "city boy." "Whatever you like. I'm all yours for a week."

"A week?" She clunked the sander into a tool box and pulled off a latex glove. "What the heck am I going to do with you for a week?"

His gaze tripped down toward her hips. *You could show me that tattoo.* "I won't get in your way."

She ran one long, slender finger over the metal,

which showed absolutely no evidence of the wreck it had been. He couldn't believe what she'd done to that dent in forty-five minutes. "You're already in my way." The mask muffled her comment, but not her trademark candor.

To her credit, she seemed to accept his arrival with more ease than he'd expected. Her initial tension subsided after a few minutes and the baby distracted them from any in-depth discussion. Callie had fussed enough to earn a bottle, which Jo administered like a pro.

When Callie had fallen asleep in the playpen, Jo had eased the bottle out of the baby's grip, cleaned it efficiently in the small sink in her office and covered her charge in a pink blanket. Then she'd pointed toward the shop, issuing a silent invitation for him to join her. He'd been sitting on the floor watching her work ever since. Far enough away to avoid sand spray, but close enough to see details.

Like the edge of that tattoo. And the gentle jiggle of her breasts every time she swiped that sander back and forth.

She hoisted herself to a stand, brushed her pants and then scooped up the handle of her tool case. "All right. That's done." Turning toward the glass-enclosed office, she peered at the baby. "She won't sleep much longer."

He rose and took the tool case from her. "Where do you keep this?"

Surprise brightened her eyes.

"Are these tools too precious for me to touch?" he asked.

"No. I'm just not used to having any help."

"I don't mean to insult your masculinity, sweetheart. I just want to get to that hike as soon as possible."

With a laugh that told him she didn't believe a word

he said, she pointed toward the opposite side of the shop. "Over there. I'll go see if she's waking up."

As he followed her instructions, he studied the shop. For a garage, it was remarkably clean, and bright with natural sunlight. There was a freshness about it—odd, considering what kind of place it was—but the work bays and tool racks all had a woman's touch to them. Not that they were pink. Just polished. Neat. Inviting, even.

Like the owner.

"You looking for code violations, counselor?"

She surprised him, having come up behind him soundlessly in her rubber-soled work boots.

"Just admiring your shop," he assured her. "It's nice. It's...feminine somehow."

Her laugh was sudden and disbelieving. "You want feminine? You should see Fluff."

Fluff? Oh, Katie's shop next door. "Maybe later," he replied. "Is Callie awake yet?"

"Any second. She's making moaning sounds. The books say I should wake her and get her on the schedule I want, but that just seems so cruel."

"You don't strike me as someone who worries what the books say."

That earned him a satisfied grin. "I don't normally. But there are so many experts on child rearing, and I want to be certain I'm doing everything right."

"I'm sure you are," he said, following her across the garage toward the office.

"Oh, there she is."

He paused and listened. "I don't hear anything."

Then he heard a faint noise that sounded like someone twisting a balloon a hundred yards away. Was that a *baby?* Jo's pace picked up as she headed toward the office. When she opened the door, the squeak became a full-force wail.

Through the glass, he could see her swoop into the baby cage and lift the tiny body. He couldn't hear Jo's words or sounds, but he imagined her crooning as she patted and cradled the squirming baby, punctuating her comments with kisses on Callie's head.

Whatever books she'd been reading couldn't teach her as much as nature had already given her. She was clearly born to be a mother.

He used to think some women just didn't know how to mother, and that's why his own abandoned the task. But now he knew he was wrong about that—wrong about his mother.

And yet here he was, twenty-six years after she bailed on her husband and sons, considering the possibility of stepping into this makeshift family and breaking it up. Just so he could heal the age-old hurt?

It didn't feel right to him. But he'd made a deal with his brothers that he would at least observe the situation and make the right decision for the child. Quinn was oddly certain that would mean bringing the baby back east to be raised by them. He and Nicole were discussing that very option this week.

And, as Cam had expected, Colin had preferred to handle their father. With his office still in Pittsburgh, Colin was closest to the older man and had kept a close eye on him. Colin had been the one to inform them that Dad had been so reclusive the past few years that he bordered on becoming a hermit.

Was that a result of decades-old guilt?

Cameron wanted to verify his mother's side of the story and trusted Colin to break the news to their dad and get *his* side of the story.

Jo interrupted his thoughts by waving him into the office, the baby apparently over her tears.

"Hey, kid," he said to the damp-eyed child when he entered, loving the little zing that went through him when her face lit up. She looked so much like Colin and Quinn at that age that he almost laughed out loud. "Do you hike, too?"

"She's a pro," Jo assured him with a glance down at his Docksiders. "It's her uncle that I'm worried about."

"I have better shoes in my rental car," he offered. "Unless you want to lend me a pair from your collection of men's boots."

She wriggled her nose and leaned into Callie's ear. "Bad uncle," she whispered.

But Callie reached her chubby little hand toward him and grabbed his nose. The sensation was almost as appealing as the chime of Jo's laughter, and the echo of her open reference to him as Callie's uncle.

"Come on," Jo said, gently tugging the baby's grip from his nose. With her free hand, she scooped up a giant bag decorated with orange bears, and indicated the door with a tilt of her head. "We'll go home first to pack a lunch. And she needs a snack."

Cam had planned to stay at one of the many bed and breakfasts he'd seen in the quaint tourist town. "I have to check in. Which one of those gingerbread places on Carvel Street do you recommend?"

"None, unless you're ready to part with way too much money. You can stay with me."

A sharp stab of temptation seized him. "With you? Are you sure?"

Her look told him she caught the implication but refused to acknowledge it. "How else are you going to see what kind of stable home environment Callie enjoys? You'll need to give a complete report to those nosy brothers of yours."

So she did understand exactly why he had come. But didn't she realize how combustible their chemistry was? Or was he the only one haunted by the memory of how her body felt underneath him?

"I appreciate the offer…" He hesitated a moment, considering how to phrase his concerns.

"I can handle it," she said, shutting down any arguments with a no-nonsense tone. "I believe you said I can handle anything."

With a long, lazy look, he took in the baby in her arms, the bag on her shoulders, the beautifully feminine hands that operated a sander with the same grace that they prepared a baby bottle. "You *can* handle anything."

But could he?

Seven

Jo checked her rearview mirror a dozen times to be sure Cam's rental car could stay with her on the twisty turns up the hillside to her house. Not that she thought there was any chance she'd *lose* him, but the sedan was no match for her four-wheel drive truck.

Of course, he was right there. Cameron McGrath wasn't going anywhere. He was one great big, hunky, sexy, charming, threatening, sexy, funny, handsome— did she say *sexy?*—fact of her life. For a week.

The thought sent a wicked shimmy through every nerve ending in her body. A *week*.

"What was I thinking inviting him to stay with us?" she asked Callie, glancing back at the baby tucked safely into the car seat in the small back seat of the truck.

Callie chewed on a blue plastic pretzel, lost in her own form of ecstasy, her eyes half-closed and a steady stream of baby drool rolling down her chin.

"You're right," Jo said with a bittersweet sigh. "I wasn't thinking. Who can *think* around that man? I practically hammered my own fingers six times while he sat there…just…" How had he been looking at her? "Eating me with his eyes."

Jo laughed at the look she got from Callie. "It's just an expression, toots. Go back to your pretzel. Pay no attention to Aunt Jo."

"Jojojojojojo."

The sound sent a bolt of happiness right through her and a sharp reminder of precisely why Jo should be thinking—and thinking hard—about the *real* reason Cameron McGrath had come to California. It had nothing to do with the electrical charge in the air when they were together and everything to do with the baby in the back.

The truck rumbled around the last turn. Through an opening of towering pine trees, she could see the white fence that lined her five acres in the mountains. At the sight of the rambling old farmhouse, a rush of security and familiarity filled her. Today, however, a different mix of sensations tugged at her heart. She was proud of the home she'd bought and restored so lovingly, but how would he see it? A man who lived in a chrome box that touched the sky?

He'd see it for the restored beauty it was, of course. A cozy two-story house with a wraparound porch, generous skylights and the finest handmade pantry in Nevada County. If he had an eye for a good carpentry job, that was.

If not, he'd see a twenty-five-year-old fixer-upper with creaky stairs, two painfully small bedrooms, a drafty chimney and a powder room in sore need of an update.

Pulling up to her closed garage door, she climbed out

of her truck and opened the back to get Callie. He parked behind her and was out and next to her before she could get the car seat unbuckled.

"You live here?"

Oh, boy. Here we go. She eased out of the cab to see the expression on his face. He was imitating her, of course, tipping back to see the tops of her trees the way she'd leaned back to see his massive skyscraper.

"No express elevator, but we call it home."

He grinned and opened the truck door wider. "Need a hand?"

"I got her." She lifted Callie from the seat and threaded the straps of her diaper bag with a free arm. When she emerged, she saw him studying the house and the heartstopping view of the white-tipped mountains that surrounded the valley beyond.

"Nice piece of real estate." The tease disappeared from his expression.

She looked around, seeing it through his eyes. Spring had left the mountains painted in lime and emerald greens, with pine forests so dense they looked black. Enormous white clouds broke the endless blue sky, casting shadows over the valley and the river that meandered through it.

"I told you my views were different." She made no attempt to mask the pride in her voice.

"You weren't kidding."

His look of approval washed over her. She wanted him to be impressed with Callie's home. She wanted him to realize what an incredible place it was to raise a child. Even though she'd been born and raised here, Jo had never gotten tired of the overwhelming beauty of the Sierra Nevadas.

She waited while he retrieved a canvas bag and a nylon-covered briefcase from his car.

"You planning on working while you're here?" she asked as they climbed the steps to the porch.

"No, the firm can easily live for a week without me signing work orders for a new supply of legal pads."

She detected a note of wistfulness in the comment. "No big cases in the works?"

He shook his head. "Not these days. I suffer from a classic syndrome. Promoted so high I don't get to do the work I love anymore. I haven't seen the inside of a courtroom in a year."

"Then why the laptop? To send daily reports back to McGrath and McGrath?"

He grinned. "They did ask if I would e-mail a picture of Callie."

Her stomach tightened as she tossed her keys and bag on the mirrored antique dresser that served as an entryway table. It was only a matter of time until they were all out here, fighting for Callie.

Burying a kiss in the folds of the baby's neck, Jo stepped aside, opting to ignore the comment. "Come on in," she said, breezing through the living room and heading to the kitchen, to what she considered the heart of her home.

In the oversize country kitchen, Callie's playpen and high chair sat near the long table under a window with a view that could double as a page from a scenic calendar.

"Wow," he said as he followed her into the kitchen, magnetically drawn to the breathtaking vista like everyone who entered the room. But he was looking at the counters, tracing a finger over her butcher block. "You're right. Not a seam in sight."

She couldn't hold back a quick laugh as she settled Callie into her high chair. "Right back there," she nodded toward the small room off the kitchen, "is a little office and guest room. You have to pull out the couch, but everyone says it's real comfortable. And you can connect your laptop into my wireless, if you like."

Aware that he watched her more than the view, she opened a container of applesauce and poured some crackers onto Callie's tray, then turned to the refrigerator to get some juice. As she did, Cameron dropped into the seat closest to the high chair. "Can I feed her?"

The request stopped her cold. Slowly, insidiously and, oh, so easily, he would worm his way into Callie's world, and then Callie would repay him by worming her way into his heart.

But Jo had invited him to see Callie's stable home, so she had only herself to blame.

"Sure," she said brightly. "You'll need a bib as much as she does, though. She might fling applesauce at your T-shirt."

"And deface the Yankee logo?" The question was more directed to Callie in tone. "You wouldn't do that, would you, sweetheart?"

Callie giggled with delight. Nice to see that all women got that melty feeling inside when he casually called them sweetheart.

"See this?" He held his arms open to give her a good look at the front of his shirt, then he pointed to the logo. Jo couldn't resist taking a peek herself. His chest was broad, the T-shirt just snug enough to show the cuts of well-defined muscles. She remembered the feel of his skin under her hands. The tickle of rough, masculine hair right over his fast-beating heart.

"This is a dynasty, kiddo," he continued to explain, unaware that his hostess's mouth had gone dry and her lower half…hadn't. Oh, boy, she was in trouble. "We can decorate your whole bedroom in Yankee colors, if you like."

"And displace the Pooh Bears I hand-stenciled?" Jo gave him an incredulous look. "You're dreamin', pal."

"Maybe not now," he agreed quickly, but added, "We can wait until after she starts to play tee ball."

Jo set a sippy cup of juice on the tray and laughed at him. "She's not going to play baseball, Cam. She's a carbon copy of her mother who would never endanger the health of a polished fingernail."

"Who knows?" He carefully scooped up a spoonful of applesauce and held it to Callie's mouth, the tiny spoon looking somehow tender and endearing in his masculine hand. "They say environment could be stronger than genes. She might be a master carpenter."

Jo felt her smile fade as she looked down at him. Was that a compliment—or a dig?

He winked at Callie, just as she opened her mouth to receive the spoonful like a perfect lady. Like she'd never thwacked a spoon of applesauce in her life. She moaned as she gummed and swallowed.

"She's really beautiful," he said softly, more to himself than to her.

Jo folded her arms and looked at Callie. "She looks so much like Katie, I could cry."

He appeared to study the applesauce closely, then asked, "I was wondering if you had any more pictures? You know, when Katie was younger?" He did a miserable job of sounding casual.

She thought of the two photo albums she and her mother had retrieved from the rubble. Every picture Chris ever took of Katie from birth to… "Yeah, I do. Lots of them."

"Maybe later I could take a look at them."

She put her hand on his shoulder, wanting to offer comfort. It had nothing to do with giving in to the urge to touch him again. "I'll show them to you tonight. After our hike."

He glanced at that hand, then looked up at her, his eyes warm, but guarded. "Where do we hike?"

She pointed out the window. "My backyard."

"That's convenient."

"Sure is. I do a couple miles almost every day."

His jaw slackened in surprise, but then he raked her with a long look that sent a hot flash through her whole body. "No wonder you're in such great shape."

The heat wave was punctuated by a flip of her heart that she vowed to ignore.

"I'm going to change, then I'll pack us some provisions," she said, pointing toward the stairs. "Think you'll be okay with her for five minutes?"

He nodded at Callie. "Of course. We'll be fine."

Jo bent down to give the baby a kiss. "I'll be right back, sugarplum."

Callie immediately looked up, that unsure expression on her face.

"Don't worry," she said softly, stroking Callie's silky dark hair. "I'm just going upstairs. You stay with…" Uncle Cam?

"Cam," he filled in for her. "She can call me Cam."

"She won't call you anything," Jo assured him. "She can't talk, Cam."

"Ca-ca-ca-ca!" Callie pointed right in his face.

His grin was pure self-satisfaction. "See that? She said my name. You watch. She'll be saying she loves me before I leave."

"That's what I'm afraid of," she admitted, trying to cover the truth with a playful laugh.

But there was nothing playful about it.

The hearts of both women in this house were officially put on notice for the following week.

Like everything else she did, Jo hiked the side of a mountain with grace, agility and ease. Callie was comfortably stashed in some sort of carrier around Jo's chest, looking out at the world, babbling and singing contentedly.

Cam easily kept up with Jo—but only because he played softball three times a week and hit the gym at the top floor of his office building on two other days. This was one serious workout.

Was it some kind of endurance test for him or was she just showing off?

From behind he studied Jo's long strides, her square shoulders, her compact backside and long, taut thighs revealed by a pair of beige hiking shorts. She could show off all she wanted—the pleasure was his. He couldn't remember ever being turned on by a woman who was so athletic and sculpted. Typically his girlfriends were bone skinny and delicate enough to blow over in a strong wind.

He tried to imagine Amanda hiking up this mountain, and the thought made him laugh out loud. Followed by a wave of relief that he'd called it quits with her before he left New York.

"Glad to hear you're having fun back there," she called over her shoulder. "'Cause things are about to get hairy."

Hairy? "Steeper, you mean?"

"Yeah. A little." She stopped and he caught up with her in two strides. She indicated *up* with one finger. Way up. "We'll go another quarter mile or so, then have lunch at my favorite spot. Unless you're too tired or hungry."

He was basically wiped out and ravenous. "I can go as long as you can," he assured her.

Her smile was half disbelief, half tease. "You don't have to prove anything to me, Cam. Just tell me if you want a break. I do this every day."

"I'm only thirty-five. I work out," he said defensively. "And I play ball."

"Uh-huh." He could have sworn her glance fluttered over his chest, but behind the sunglasses she wore it was hard to be sure. It wouldn't be the first time he'd caught her checking him out. She'd been drooling more than Callie in the kitchen.

"Come on, tomgirl," he tapped her shoulder playfully. "Keep hiking."

"Tomgirl?" She laughed. "Where'd you get that one?"

He pulled his own sunglasses down far enough to be sure she saw the look of sincerity in his eyes. "You're too female to qualify as a tom*boy.*"

He couldn't see her eyes, but the rush of color to her face had nothing to do with the warm California sun that baked down on them.

She turned around and headed back up the hillside. "Watch your step, then," she said, and whispered something to Callie he didn't catch.

About an hour later they stopped at a wide clearing of grass surrounded by pines so thick they practically obliterated the blue sky. The air was thin and crispy clean, whispering through the pine needles like mother nature's even breathing.

"So this is your favorite spot, huh?" Cam tugged off the knapsack he'd offered to carry, taking in the storybook quality of the view.

"It sure is. In the whole world."

In what seemed like no time, she'd spread a blanket,

put out some food and drinks and set the baby in the middle of it all. No matter what she did, Jo had one eye on the child and could grab her before she'd crawled an inch out of her spot.

These two ladies seemed to communicate wordlessly.

A twinge of guilt twisted his gut. It would be a damn travesty to break them up.

He settled onto an edge of the blanket, his gaze torn between the natural beauty of the world around him… and the woman in front of him.

"So what's the legal order of events for adoption?" he asked.

Jo looked up from the container of fruit she was opening, shrugging her shoulder to push back a strand of reddish brown hair that escaped her ponytail. "I have a meeting on Friday with Child Services."

"What's on the agenda?"

She held out the container. "Want a strawberry?"

He took one and nodded thanks, then she offered the dish to Callie, who sat cross-legged between them. "Strawberry, Cal?"

The baby grabbed a fat berry and began to gnaw on it, while Cam waited for Jo to answer his question.

"It was supposed to be the meeting where I presented them with the signed Petition of Relinquishment. But, now…" She popped a slice of cantaloupe into her mouth and looked away.

Now…she had no signature.

"Are they expecting a signed petition?"

She shook her head and answered after she'd swallowed. "They don't know you exist. I wanted to hit them with the news and your formal consent at the same time."

He lay down, leaning on his elbow to watch her wipe some pink slobber from Callie's chin.

"I gotta hand it to you, Jo," he said. "You don't whine. You haven't cried or stomped your foot or pleaded with me to go home."

She smiled wistfully. "I learned a long time ago how ineffective those techniques are."

Somehow, he just *knew* where she'd learned that lesson. "Katie?"

"She gave a new meaning to a fine California whine."

He laughed at that, and accepted the hunk of French bread she offered to him.

"She does sound like a pain in the butt."

"Yeah, but she was *my* pain in the butt. So I loved her." She leaned back on her hands and dropped her head back so that the sun washed her face. "And I miss her whining like you can't believe."

He had to fight the urge to reach over the blanket and touch the sliver of silky skin exposed at the V-neck of her simple, white T-shirt. Suddenly he remembered what that skin tasted like, how hot and slick her flesh had been under his mouth. Her thick, auburn ponytail nearly brushed the ground behind her and his fingers ached to get back into that mane of hair.

"I'll go with you." He had no idea where that announcement had come from, but he accepted it as right.

"Excuse me?" She sat straight and looked at him, lifting her sunglasses to peer at him. "You'll go with me to the Child Services meeting?"

"Yep."

"Why would you do that?"

"Aren't you planning to tell them about us—about my family—at that meeting?"

She nodded. "Not that they'll believe the story, but, yes, I have to."

She *didn't* have to, and he knew it. She could have

easily concealed the fact that Callie had living relatives and moved forward with the adoption. The fact that she hadn't, that she'd made a concerted effort to find him and do everything the right way continued to amaze him, and he liked her for the honesty.

"If I'm there to corroborate your story, will that help or hurt?"

"It might expedite things. Either way, they'll launch a full-scale investigation and interview you, and probably your brothers."

He knew why, of course. He'd investigated California adoption laws the minute Jo had left New York. Without a will stipulating custody and care, Callie was legally his or his brothers, because the familial rights were considered stronger than close friends.

But that's where the law got dicey. Callie could remain in Jo's custody, but the consent to give her up for adoption fell to him. There were few cases with similar precedents, but in every one the child had ended up with the living relatives by order of the court. The legal cards were stacked against Jo.

Callie rolled over onto all fours and launched into a speed crawl. At the same time, they lunged for her, their hands and bodies touching as they reached her at the precise same moment. He backed off and let Jo take her.

Which, he knew, was exactly what he should do with the whole adoption process. From the look Jo gave him, she was thinking the same thing.

"The woman we'll meet with is Mary Beth Borrell," she said, easing Callie back and giving her some bread. "What are you going to tell her?"

"I'll tell them I'm here to observe. To make sure Callie is safe and loved."

"And then? Will you…" She cleared her throat and

smiled at him. "I really *don't* want to whine when I ask this question. But will you sign the petition, then?"

"I can't, Jo."

He saw her delicate jaw slacken.

"I can't until I've discussed it with my brothers. We each have our tasks this week, then we'll decide what to do."

"Your tasks?"

He nodded. "Colin is talking to our dad, to tell him what happened and, hopefully, to get the truth about the past."

"We already know the truth."

He didn't respond to that. "Quinn is…" He hated to tell her this. "Quinn and Nicole are discussing the possibility of taking on another child, since they are already expecting one."

She blew out a disgusted breath. "Great. That's just great. And you're here to test my mothering skills."

He reached over and put his hand on top of hers. "There's nothing to test, Jo. You're a wonderful mother. Callie's lucky to have you."

She surprised him by turning her hand over and lacing her fingers through his. "Tell that to Child Services."

"I intend to."

But Cam knew that Child Services wasn't Jo's problem. It was his brothers who had gone from lukewarm to burning hot on the idea that their sister's baby should be part of the family. That Callie's "destiny" was to heal the hurt caused by their parent's ancient and stupid actions.

He knew what Quinn and Nicole would want to do. And Colin was just rebellious enough to do the polar opposite of whatever Dad thought was right.

Even if he disagreed, his brothers had an equal say in the fate of Callie McGrath.

Jo's fingers felt warm and oddly comforting. They were slender and smooth and strong. The capable hands of a collision-repair expert.

Good thing. Because he could easily be the cause of the next major wreck in her life.

Eight

From his comfortable position in the corner of her sofa, Cameron turned to the last page of the photo album, and a grin broke across his face. Even though Jo sat on the floor by the hearth, curled under her favorite blanket while he studied the pictures, she knew why he was smiling. She had added the last shot from her own collection.

The photo had been taken in Reno, just a week before the earthquake. Jo could see it in her mind's eye— Katie beaming underneath the famous arched "Reno" sign, holding a pair of strappy black stilettos in one hand and her cowboy hat in the other.

"But she's wearing shoes," he noted. "Why is she holding a pair?"

"The ones she's holding are mine," Jo said.

That got a surprised look. "No way."

"Way." She laughed softly.

A killer smile spread over his face. "I'd pay big bucks to see you in those shoes."

Her whole lower half nearly melted in a puddle at the implication in his voice. "Yeah. Well. I don't wear them often. I bought her the hat and had it monogrammed with her nickname as a birthday present. While we were waiting for the monogram to be done, we went shoe shopping and she picked those for me."

He studied the picture closely. "She looks really happy."

"She was. Things had settled down. Roger Morgan—that's Callie's father—moved away from Sierra Springs. Buff 'n' Fluff was finally starting to make money. Things were good."

"That didn't last long," he noted.

"Nope. Nature stepped in and did a major shake up."

He closed the book with a thud.

Callie had fallen asleep right after dinner, and Jo and Cameron had been talking ever since. For Jo, the night could have gone on forever. He was easy to talk to, funny and smart. Looking at him bordered on sinful, it was so pleasurable. And he teased her just enough to keep her on edge and tingly.

But something had bothered her while he'd studied the pictures, and she decided it was time to ask. "Why don't you make any comments about your mother?"

He shrugged. "What's to say? She looked good. Pretty youthful. She aged better than my dad, I'll tell you that."

"He has guilt on his conscience."

That made him laugh, oddly enough.

"Do you think that's funny?"

"No." He shook his head, still smiling. "It's just that that's exactly what my Gram McGrath would have said.

She was always saying things like that about all of us. She had a prediction or a fateful pronouncement for every man in the McGrath family."

Jo pulled the blanket higher, as the cool evening air wafted through the drafty chimney next to her. "What did she say?"

"She said Dad's guilty conscience would do him in someday, but only when he wasn't around. He didn't like to hear that."

"And now you know why," she said.

He placed the photo album on the coffee table and leaned back into the sofa. "I guess I do."

"What about you and your brothers? What did your grandmother say?"

"Well, let's see. Quinn is, or was, a pretty serious babe magnet."

"Like you're not."

He chuckled. "Let's just say he elevated it to an art form. Anyway, she used to say he'd find 'the one' and settle down."

"And she was right?"

He nodded. "You should see him with Nic. Happy as a pig in…Florida. She always said Colin was the lucky one, born to get things easily."

"Does he?"

"He has a great girl, a successful company. He made it look easy, even if it wasn't."

"And what about you? What did your Gram say was your fate in life?"

His smile disappeared, and that sent a shiver of worry through Jo. "Tell me," she urged.

He suddenly stood up. "Just an old Irish lass musing, Jo. Nothing to take seriously." He stretched, drawing her attention to that damn Yankee logo again. "I think I'm going to take a shower and turn in. The time change has caught up with me."

Whatever his grandmother had predicted for Cam was going to remain a secret.

"You have to use my shower upstairs," she said. "The bathroom down here is just a powder room."

"What, you haven't installed a shower with your bare hands in your spare time?" He reached down to pull her up, easily lifting her to her feet.

"It's on my to-do list," she assured him, releasing her hand even though she didn't want to.

When they got to the top of the stairs, she pointed to her bedroom. "I'll be in here."

"Getting your pj's on?" He wiggled his eyebrows playfully.

"I don't—"

"I know you don't." He winked at her. "That's why I suggested it."

"Very funny." She tapped his shoulder, pushing him toward the bathroom. "I do make special exceptions."

While he showered, Jo changed into the only sleep-wear she could muster, Sponge Bob SquarePants boxer shorts and a tank top. Then she remembered she should make up the sofa bed...or Cam might be tempted to crawl into hers.

With a shiver of mixed feelings, she slipped back downstairs, determined to open the bed, make it up with clean sheets and be back safe in her own room before he finished his shower.

She didn't want to hang around any room that contained a bed *and* Cam McGrath. It was a deadly combination.

"Can I see your tattoo?"

She spun around, caught by surprise. How did he get down the stairs without creaking a single step?

And, how, dear God, could she be expected to breathe with him standing in the doorway, shirtless and in drawstring pants, his wet hair dripping rivulets down his muscular chest?

And how the heck did he know she had a tattoo?

He laughed. "I've rendered you speechless."

Shaking her head in a vain effort to rattle sense back into it, she laughed lightly. "No, you can't see my tattoo."

He crossed his arms and grinned. "I already saw the tip of it when you were hammering that Toyota. It's red. Dark. In a very interesting place."

A rush of blood warmed her face. "It's private. No one but the tattoo artist has ever seen it. And Katie."

"Special occasion?"

"Yeah. I got it when I…" Oh, she'd never hear the end of it from him. "I accomplished something after several years of work."

He stepped into the room, filling it with his utterly sinful, completely uncovered, perfectly shaped, slightly hairy, totally touchable chest.

Jeez. He might as well wear a sign: Danger Ahead.

"Do you mind?" she asked, sidestepping him as he got closer.

"Uh, I think this is my room. I have to come in here eventually." His grin was just as deadly as his chest, leaving her nowhere to look. "Come on, Jo," he whispered mischievously, glancing down at her hip. "Let me see it."

She backed up, hating the heat that made her whole body shaky and damp, but loving the interplay and flirting. Talk about elevating the chase to an art form. The man was a pro.

"No. You can't see it."

"Then tell me what you accomplished to earn it."

He'd never give up.

"Follow me," she said, slipping past him. "But leave the door to the garage open so I can hear if Callie calls me."

"We're going into the garage?"

She glanced over her shoulder. "Where else would you expect to find something I accomplished?"

She heard him chuckle as she padded barefoot through the kitchen to the garage door. She opened the heavy wooden door slowly, so the creak wouldn't wake Callie, and walked through the pitch-black to the work lamp she kept on the other side.

"Where'd you go?" he asked. "What is—"

He just stopped talking and stared. For a long, lovely minute, he just stared at her pride and joy.

"Now I've rendered you speechless," she said with a smile, then ran her hand along the gleaming red hood of the Mustang. "Isn't she gorgeous?"

He whistled in appreciation. "Yeah. Sixty-five. The second year it was made." Approaching it slowly and with just the appropriate amount of reverence, he crouched down to look at one of the wheels, touching the rims gently. "What beautiful lines." Bless him for noticing the details.

"When I found it, there was almost nothing usable on it. The car had been totaled by a truck and left as a wreck in a junkyard."

He looked up from the wheel base. "You restored a totaled, forty-year-old Mustang?" His look of awe gave her more confidence than if he'd stared at her naked and praised her to the sky.

"This was my life, before Callie." She pinched the tip of the hood ornament with affection. "I spent more than two years of Sundays working on this car. Don't you love the color?"

"Like a candy apple."

She smiled at that. "Yep. And just as sweet."

"Did you rebuild the engine?"

She shook her head. "How many times do I have to tell you I'm not a mechanic? A friend of mine did it." She reached for the release and lifted the hood. "It gleams on the inside, too."

He moved closer to her, pinning her between the open hood and his still only half-dressed body. "This car's as pretty as you are."

Her heart walloped against her chest. His sheer, undressed proximity destabilized her, and she curled her fingers around the front end of the car to keep from giving in to the weakness in her knees.

"Why are you doing this?" she managed to ask.

He didn't answer for a minute, and she half expected him to play dumb and give her a "doing what?" in response.

"Because I've been dying to kiss you all day." Why would she expect anything but abject honesty from this man? "Haven't you?" he asked.

And didn't he deserve honesty in return? "Yes."

He covered her mouth with his in an instant, his powerful arms pulling her right into that very chest she'd been admiring. She locked her arms behind his neck and melted into his kiss.

He eased against her, a soft moan from his throat matching the one from hers. His lips burned a path down her throat, and his right hand followed the same trail.

Blood coursed through her veins at breakneck speed, rushing from her head to the center of her, already throbbing and needy. Not a single cell in her body had the strength or will to fight him. This was too good. Too amazing. Too *right*.

He bent over to kiss the skin of her throat, dipping to the rise of her breasts. All she could do was hold his head, inhale the clean scent of his wet hair and press him against her body and heart.

With one hand he held her tightly into him, his erection jamming against her lower belly. The other hand slid under her tank top and glided up her body until it covered her breast.

She sucked in a jagged, anxious breath, and he kissed her mouth again, hungry and hot, his tongue delving deep into her, his thumb rubbing her nipple to an achy, painful, precious hardness.

He pulled away from her, his gaze darting toward the car. "How 'bout the back seat? It was made for this, you know."

She shook her head and tried to look suitably shocked at the suggestion. Even though it had definite appeal. "Not in my car. No way." She attempted to pull away from him, but he wouldn't release her.

"Then come back in the house." He tugged her forward and closed the hood with one hand. Keeping one arm tightly around her waist, he ushered her into the house, and the minute he had her in the kitchen, he eased her against the door to the garage and sought out another anxious kiss.

"I…I can't…" She tried to speak, but she could only groan, her eyes closed, her hips moving. "I can't stop," she managed.

He laughed low and sexy in her ear. "Then don't."

Kissing the bare skin of her shoulder, he ran his hands down her back until he held her backside. She grabbed his head and pulled him to her mouth, smothering her doubts with a lip-crunching kiss. Her whole body hummed with the sensations flying through her.

In one quick move, he lifted her off her feet. "Let's see what we can do on your seamless countertops."

He set her gently on the counter and slid his hips right between her legs. The only illumination was from the moon, and a soft light that spilled from the guest room into one corner of the kitchen.

She clung to his shoulders, his wide, wonderful, masculine shoulders, as he kissed her again, their faces now at the same level. Then he bent his head and suckled the exposed skin above her breasts, sending more fireworks straight to the center of her.

"What am I doing up here?" she asked, half laughing, half serious.

"I'm looking for something," he whispered, then dipped under her arm. Before she realized what he was doing, he tugged gently at the waistband of her boxers, pulling them down over her hip and the top of her behind. Then he lowered his head to her hip and flicked her skin with his tongue.

He stopped, long enough to look at the tattoo, then placed his lips on her and kissed her flesh so long and so sweet, she thought he must be able to taste the ink that formed the galloping horse. Finally, slowly, he stood up in front of her.

"A Mustang, of course," he said, shaking his head. "My girl's got a car logo on her sweet little behind."

His *girl?* Well, his girl of the moment. Of the evening. Maybe even the week. "I'm not anyone's girl."

He burrowed his fingers into the hair at the nape of her neck, gently easing the ponytail holder out and freeing her hair. "No, you're not."

A twinge of disappointment tickled her.

"You are your *own* girl, Jo Ellen." His voice was raspy with arousal and a hint of tenderness. He guided her against his erection and leaned into her ear to whisper, "And I like that best about you."

Unable to stop herself, she pushed her hips harder against him as every nerve ending in her sang with pleasure and the need for more. Moisture covered her skin as she sucked in the air around him, the soapy, delicious smell of him just making her want him worse.

Their tongues tangled as he eased his hands back under her shirt and slowly, mercilessly, caressed her breasts again. Pulling her shirt all the way up, he dipped his head and took one nipple into his mouth, sucking and teasing it before moving to the other one. His teeth gently tweaked her, sending fire from her breasts to her core, making her rock against him.

Making her forget she was on her very own butcher block kitchen counter.

And loving it.

She almost collapsed at the thought of it. "Are we really going to do this here? On my counter?"

"Wherever you want, sweetheart." He kissed her, and tugged her lower lip between his teeth before releasing it. "Here, there, upstairs." He blazed a trail of kisses down her throat. "In the car. On the roof. In the grass."

His hand slipped inside her boxer shorts again, sliding to the front and causing her to practically spasm in anticipation of his touch.

"I don't care where the hell we go," he continued as he dipped his fingers closer to the tuft of hair between her legs. "I just have to make love to you. I have to taste you. I have to be inside of you."

She took one ragged breath, prepared to agree to anything, anywhere, when Callie's wail interrupted everything.

* * *

Cam followed Jo's cute little butt up the stairs, resisting the urge to yank down the ridiculous underwear and eat that Mustang tattoo. But the body shop calendar girl had disappeared and a caring mother took her place.

He wanted to curse the little demon who broke their rhythm, but he couldn't even bring himself to be mad when he saw the scrunched up red face in the glow of the night-light. She stood in the crib, her little legs marching in place as though she could simply climb out and get whatever she wanted.

And she wanted Jo.

The instant Jo scooped her up and started cooing in her ear, the crying subsided.

"She needs a bottle," Jo said.

"I'll get it."

"No, no. At night it has to be warm, and my microwave is touchy."

"Jo, I can warm a bottle of milk, for crying out loud."

She held the tiny body out to him. "Here. Just rock her for a minute, I'll be right back."

Before he could respond, he was holding the baby who let out an indignant whimper at the transfer of power.

"Okay, we can do this." He dropped into the rocking chair in the corner of the tiny room and fumbled to get her in a comfortable position, finally settling her into a half stand against his chest. How had he gone from holding one sexy grown-up woman sighing for his kisses to one miniature peanut shuddering for a bottle—in the space of two minutes?

"Hey, kid." He stroked her black curls the way he'd seen Jo do. "Your timing sucks. I mean, stinks. Your timing stinks."

She shuddered and slumped her head right into the

corner of his shoulder and neck. An entirely different sensation of *wholeness* danced through him. Of course, he'd much rather feel *whole* with Jo's legs wrapped around his hips and her delicate breasts under his hands, but as good feelings went, this was a close second.

"You probably sensed that something big was going on downstairs, didn't you?"

She moaned softly, then sighed.

"Aw, come on, kid. I'm not planning to take her away from you. Or you from her, for that matter." He scooted her a little higher, loving that little head on his shoulder. But what *was* he doing making love to Jo Ellen Tremaine?

He just wanted her. Pure and plain lust. Why would it have to be more than that? She was a smart, accomplished, dynamic and strong woman with a very, very seductive body and face.

Was it more than that?

Nah. He liked her, of course. But he wanted her. This was lust, a healthy, controllable, familiar response to a woman. It was just...*strong* lust.

He hadn't made it through a minute and a half since he met her without imagining himself kissing her, touching her, plunging inside of her. And he'd been so close. And she'd been so ready—

"Here we go."

His eyes flew open at the sound of her voice. She stood in front of him, holding a bottle and a blanket, reaching toward Callie.

"I'll do it," he insisted. "We're too comfortable to move now."

To her credit, she didn't argue. She just handed him the bottle and some instinct made him ease Callie into the crook of his arm. Jo draped the baby in the blanket and leaned over.

He expected her to kiss Callie, but instead her lips gently grazed his cheek, then she surprised him even further by curling up on the floor next to them. Wordlessly she laid her head on his knee.

Now he had two women on him. Two beautiful women trusting him with their affection. Two amazing women whose futures he held in his hand, to be changed with a single pen stroke.

If he really liked Jo, he'd give her what she wanted. Assurance that she could adopt Callie.

With Callie in his elbow, holding her own bottle, he reached his free hand to gently stroke Jo's hair as it fell over his leg. She sighed softly.

And suddenly, an intense sensation of déjà vu washed over him so sharply, he could hardly breathe. He'd been here before. Only *he* was the one who sat at a woman's knee while a baby got a bottle.

He remembered. Oh God, he remembered her so clearly. He could smell the mix of formula and flowers, feel the skin of her fingers as she stroked his hair.

He waited for the old burst of pain, but for the first time since he was nine years old, it didn't come. He no longer hated her for leaving. It was time to give his mother the benefit of the doubt. And that, he knew, was what healing the family was all about.

And if he was "healed," so, too, would Colin and Quinn be. They didn't need to break up this tiny family. This baby wasn't their salvation. That came from the knowledge that their mother really had loved them.

And Jo had given that to him. That must be why it felt like "more than" lust. And he had to repay her for that gift.

"Jo," he whispered, hoping Callie's closed eyes didn't flutter open.

Jo lifted her head and looked up at him.

"I want to sign the paper."

She narrowed her eyes in disbelief. "Because you want to sleep with me?"

He smiled at her. "No. I do, but that's not why I'm going to sign it. I want to do the right thing. I'll do everything I can to be sure she stays with you."

"But what about your brothers? Would you take them on, if they fight it?"

He hated the thought. "I never have. We've never disagreed about anything that matters. The three of us have always been united." He looked down and gently tugged the bottle out of Callie's slackened lips. "But I will fight them on this if I have to." Maybe he wouldn't have to.

Jo slowly rose to her knees, positioning herself in front of him and the baby. Then she reached up and cradled his face in her hands. At her touch, he closed his eyes and let out a slow, soft breath.

"I'm sorry, Cam. I'm sorry if this makes more pain for your family."

He opened his eyes, and looked at her. "My grandma also said I was born to do the right thing."

"Do you know what the right thing is in this case?" Her voice was barely a whisper.

He nodded. "Callie has to stay with you."

"Oh." It sounded like a little sob. "Thank you."

Between them, the baby nestled deeper into his arm and whimpered contentedly. Cam looked down at her and silently agreed with the sentiment. He'd never known such contentment. *Never.*

"No. Thank *you*," he whispered to Jo.

She just nodded, and reached for the baby. "I'll change her diaper and put her down. My room's across the hall. I'll be there in two minutes."

Her message was completely clear.

Nine

Cam left a single lamp burning in the tiny room. Because he wanted to see Jo, wanted to watch her come undone under his hands and mouth and body. He wanted to see her face when he thanked her for the gift she'd given him. If she hadn't come forward, if she hadn't made the effort to do the "right" thing, he never would have known the truth about his mother. He never would have been released from his old enemy.

Of course, if he told her that, she'd turn into Sigmund Freud and claim they were making love as some kind of gratitude-comfort-whole-earth-natural healing stuff.

And that wasn't the case. His body simply ached with need and want and a singular craving to be inside of her.

He slid under her covers, inhaling the powdery scent he recognized as hers, and yanked off his drawstring pants. He'd make short order of those cartoon-decorated boxer shorts the minute she was in bed with him.

He smiled at the thought. Who ever thought he'd be aching to get inside a cowgirl-mechanic-carpenter-tomboy-hiker who wore boxer shorts and had a tattoo of a horse?

But just thinking about her made him harder. Where *was* she? He closed his eyes and wrapped an arm around her pillow, imagining it was her. Two minutes, she'd said. Come on, sweetheart.

He closed his eyes and ignored the fact that it was about three in the morning in New York. He couldn't possibly fall asleep with this erection and that woman under the same roof.

He breathed in her fragrance. Imagined her naked underneath him. Tasted her sweet skin, her soft lips, the flesh of her breasts….

Cam heard voices. Women's voices. Soft laughter. The sound of a cup hitting a saucer. A baby squealing and women talking.

He pulled himself out of the deepest, soundest sleep he could remember, unable to fathom where he could be that would include the sound of women laughing.

He blinked and looked around. Thick, carved mahogany bedposts blocked his view.

He was in Jo's room. He flattened his palm against the empty pillow next to him, a thud of disappointment hitting his stomach.

Who was she talking to? He squinted into the light—morning light—not the lamp he'd left on—and peered at the clock on her nightstand. *Seven o'clock?*

He swore under his breath.

Running a hand through his hair and over his unshaven face, he weighed his options. The only one that made sense was to wait for her to come back up here.

Had she ever been here? The bed was rumpled, all

over. Evidence that two people had slept in it. Had he held her all night and slept right through it?

Damn every single time zone.

He started to throw off the covers, then stopped. Regardless of who was with her, she probably wouldn't want him to come stumbling into the kitchen like he'd had his way with her.

Even if he hadn't.

He could have sworn he heard her voice call, "Bye!" just as a door slammed downstairs.

Pulling himself up, he made it to the window in one stride. He shoved back the lacy drapes in time to see the rear of her big-ass truck roll past the fence and out of sight.

A dish clanged in the kitchen sink and the baby called out "Jojojojojojo!"

Who the hell was down there?

Curiosity beat good manners as he brushed his teeth in the upstairs bathroom, pulled on the pants and T-shirt he'd left hanging on the back of the door, and headed for the kitchen, not at all sure what he'd find.

"Ah, hello," he said to the back of a woman who stood at the sink.

She whirled around, training eyes the same color as Jo's directly on him. For a long moment she just stared at him and he took in her features. She was around sixty, but her skin glowed with the same luminescence as Jo's. Her short hair was a mix of white and dark red, her face lined, but finely chiseled.

One good look left him no doubt this was Jo's mother.

"She said you looked like a movie star."

He blinked. "She did?" He couldn't imagine Jo using the expression about anyone, even the man who'd slept next to her all night.

"Well, she said you *would.* When you grew up." Wiping her hands on a towel, the woman walked toward him. "I'm Alice Tremaine."

When he *grew up?*

Oh. *Oh.* Of course. His mother. "So I guess you already know who I am."

"Cameron. The serious one."

He felt the air escaping his chest in a long, agonizing sigh. Did he want to know this? Would it make him feel better, or worse? He shook her hand quickly, then pulled away.

"Where's Jo?" he asked, purposely walking to Callie's playpen. He reached down with a grin and gave her his index finger to tug. "Hey, kid. How'd ya sleep?"

He felt Alice's piercing gaze follow him. "She went to work. I was planning on taking Callie to my house. I usually have her for a few days each week, so Jo can catch up. But now we're not sure if I should take her. She said to leave it up to you."

He imagined the house without a baby. A house with no interruptions. "Don't change your plans on my account. I'll be here for a while."

How had Jo explained to her mother that he'd spent the night upstairs? Obviously, it wasn't an issue. She looked hard at him, but she hadn't whipped out a handgun and demanded he marry her daughter.

"She said if any of her sons ever wanted to find her, it would be you." She again. *Mom.*

He raked his hand through his hair. Did he really want to hear this?

She took a step closer, her gaze judgmental. A petite woman, she had to look way up at him. But that didn't seem to intimidate her. "She never could believe that you wouldn't give her a chance to tell her side."

He held up his hands as if he could stop her. "And I'm sorry about that. It's ancient history, Miss, Mrs—"

"Al. Everyone calls me Al. Like Jo. We have boys' names."

He nodded. He'd call her anything not to have this conversation. "I read the letters, Al. I know what happened. I can't change history and you probably know my dad did a pretty good job of creating it."

"Then why are you here?" Her bronze eyes held that same demand as Jo's. A look a person couldn't ignore.

"I came here to meet Callie. To see her home. To make sure she's safe and fine." If there were more underlying reasons, he sure as hell wasn't about to tell her.

"You came here to find out about your mother."

"And I have," he explained slowly. "My interest is in the well-being of my niece. Now I know she is cared for and loved, I have to figure out a way to be sure Callie can stay with Jo."

Did he even owe this woman an explanation? Yes, he did. Because she'd befriended his mother. Because she'd taken in a pregnant woman who'd been turned out of her own home.

"Then you're willing to go against your mother's wishes."

He looked sharply at her. "My—what do you mean?"

"Because Chris left a will. An explicit, detailed will and testament."

"Excuse me?"

"In it, she left everything to you."

His gut knotted. "Well, I don't really want anything, so perhaps you could arrange to give whatever she left to her favorite charity."

"You can't give Callie to charity."

Callie? "I'm afraid I don't follow you."

"Chris stipulated quite clearly that if anything ever happened to Katie, and Callie was in her care, she wanted *you* to raise her." At his look of sheer disbelief, she added, "She had a constant worry about Katie running off or doing something wild. She worried about Callie's welfare so much."

For a moment he wondered if he were in the middle of his own earthquake. Surely the world shifted, and that's what made him almost lose his balance. "Even if she did, it's a moot point because they died at the same time."

"No, they didn't," she corrected him. "Chris was taken to a hospital and died five hours after Katie. For those five hours, technically, Callie was in Chris's care."

He tried to process the facts, thinking like a lawyer, but the man in him took over for the moment. "Why didn't Jo tell me that?"

"She doesn't know the will exists. I'm the only person who has seen a copy of it."

Was this a dream? Was he still upstairs in that cozy four poster bed, sleeping off jet lag and a middle-of-the-night wake-up call by a baby?

"When were you going to tell her?" he managed to ask.

"I'm not. The will says that I could only tell you. In person. Not over the phone and not by mail. I've been waiting for you to show up."

"And what if I hadn't?"

"I had no doubt you would."

"How'd you know that?"

She shrugged narrow shoulders. "Women's intuition. Gut feeling. Knowing your mother as well as I did."

"But what if I had just signed the paper in New York, and never saw Jo again?"

She reached over for a handbag that sat on a kitchen table. From it she pulled a long, thin sheet of paper with the familiar airline logo visible. "My ticket to New York." Then she took out another piece of paper, letter size, folded in threes. "And the last will and testament of Christine McGrath. Your signature on that petition is meaningless until this goes through probate."

There went another aftershock.

If what she said was true, then he not only had to take on Quinn and Colin but the final wishes of his mother, too.

"Sit down, Cameron." She pulled a chair out from the kitchen table. "I have a message from your mother."

Jo gunned the truck up the last hill, anxious to get home after a morning's work. She'd turned the Toyota over to its happy owner and taken on one more job for the week. After that, she'd closed the shop and headed for home. For Cam.

Hopefully he'd had enough sleep and agreed to let her mom take Callie for a few days. Her lips lifted in a wicked smile. Yep. He needed that long night's sleep, because she planned to make him very, very tired.

Any doubts she had about making love to him disappeared as she'd held him in her arms all night. He slept so deeply and soundly, like a man at peace with himself. She refused to be insulted that he crashed before they'd made love. The time difference was rough, and he seemed to need sleep more than sex.

Although when she thought of his male hardness against her most of the night, he seemed to need sex pretty badly, too. A splash of adrenaline mixed with her already-frothed-up hormones, making her slam the gas pedal and spew some dirt from her back tires.

As she rounded the bend, her heart dropped. The white rental car was gone, and her little farmhouse looked…empty. Inside, her observations were confirmed. He was gone.

With a sharp pain in her chest, she rushed into the back office. His bag was gone. The sofa bed was made. In a minor state of panic, she searched all over the downstairs for a note. An explanation. Even the signed petition, though she hated herself for even thinking that.

He'd just *left?*

She stood in the middle of her kitchen trying not to let the waves of resentment and disillusionment roll over her.

Men leave.

Don't they?

She glanced around and saw that the bag she'd packed for Callie was also gone, along with her toys and several bottles. Her mother had taken all of that with her.

Had they talked first? Had her mother told him something that made him pack up and run? She tried calling Alice's number but got the machine.

Hanging up with a disgusted grunt, she grabbed a bottle of water from the pantry, yanked on a baseball cap and sunglasses that hung by the back door and headed out to the mountain to hike.

For a good hour she didn't think. She just moved. One foot in front of the other, one step at a time, a sheen of perspiration forming over her warm skin. She watched her booted feet navigate each rock on her path up the mountain, listening only to the song of one of the gray warblers who nested in the live oak and birch trees, trying, but failing, to ignore the self-chastisement and questions in her head.

She'd been more than ready to sleep with him. She wanted him. Like she hadn't wanted anyone or anything in years. She liked him. Respected him. Melted right into his hard male body all night and fantasized about the moment he would enter her.

And he'd left. Maybe he'd just gone into town.

Maybe not. Men, after all, leave. Usually after sex; but he could be different in that regard. No, they leave. Her father left. Her husband left. Women, on the other hand, stay forever.

Unless Mother Nature steps in.

She forced herself to climb, sucking in the pine-fresh air, and pushing her hat back to let the sunshine that dappled through the trees warm her face.

And she wouldn't even *think* about the petition he'd promised to sign. The brothers he promised to fight. The lovemaking he'd promised in the car, on the counter and in the grass. *Damn* him.

And suddenly like a vision from heaven, there he was. Lying on his back in the middle of her clearing, one leg bent, his hands behind his head, his eyes closed.

Cam.

He hadn't left. He'd come back to her secret place. She froze like a deer sighting a hunter and stared at him, unable to speak until her pulse slowed to a normal rate.

"What are you doing here?" she finally asked.

If the sound of her voice startled him, he never flinched to show it. "Thinking."

"Thinking?" All kinds of relief flooded her, and she had to force herself to walk toward him instead of run.

She stood next to him, looking down at his long, lean body. He wore a white T-shirt with a dark green *F* over the pocket and the words Futura Investments underneath. Her gaze traveled over his faded jeans, and the boots he'd hiked in yesterday. There was no blanket or knapsack in sight.

"What are you thinking about?"

He squinted up at her. "I'm a wreck, Jo."

She dropped to her knees. "Well, lucky you," she said softly, reaching out to smooth his tousled hair. "Wrecks are my specialty."

He smiled and closed his eyes. "I met your mother."

"And she wrecked you?"

He laughed lightly. "Not intentionally."

Somehow she understood. He'd finally come to terms with the real truth behind his mother's disappearance. All those years he'd misjudged her, hated her even. Now he had to adjust to a new history. That couldn't be easy.

But she could help him. She could fix him. She could…love him. Figuratively speaking. She'd start with the truth. "I thought you left."

He leaned up on one elbow. "What?"

"I didn't see your car or your bags and…I thought you went back to New York."

"My bag is up in your room," he said slowly, his midnight-blue gaze studying her carefully. "Was that presumptuous of me?"

She shook her head, absolutely hating the overdose of relief that wouldn't stop soaring through her. "No. That's fine. That's exactly where I want it."

"I parked my car behind your garage."

"Oh. I didn't see it." She hadn't even looked. She'd just assumed he was gone.

He reached up to her face and caressed the line of her jaw. "Sorry I fell asleep last night."

She loved the strength of his fingertips. "So was I."

"You should have woken me up." He inched her face closer.

"You were dead, honestly. I didn't have the heart."

He regarded her for a moment. "You have plenty of heart, Jo Ellen."

She bent toward him. "I'm so glad you didn't leave," she admitted.

"I told you I'm yours for a week." He reached up and took off her hat. "Come here and kiss me, tomgirl."

She needed no more encouragement.

Their kiss was just as hungry as the night before, but he seemed different somehow. He seemed more connected to her, more tender emotion and less raw sexuality. Or was that her imagination?

She unfolded herself onto the grass next to him, loving the aroma of her mountains that clung to his skin and clothes. Still kissing, he pulled her on top of him, and she straddled him, positioning him between her legs as a natural, easy rhythm started between their hips.

Released from the cap, her hair fell down her shoulders, around his face. He turned into it, inhaling, his hands on her head, her back, over her buttocks. With little effort he rolled over and locked her under him, between his thighs.

Her arms stayed around his neck, but he supported himself with one hand on the ground. With the other, he reached toward her cotton blouse. "You got all dressed up today, Jo."

Khakis and a button-down shirt? Well, he'd never seen her in anything but jeans and T-shirts. And boxer shorts. "I had to meet with a customer."

He unfastened the first button and she held her breath.

"Anybody ever come up here?" he asked.

She shook her head. "Nope. This place is all mine. I own it."

His eyes widened. "You own it?"

"Yep. My mountain. My stream. My trees."

He kissed her. "My *goodness,*" he continued in the

same beat, then made short order of the next two buttons. "You're beautiful, smart, accomplished, sexy and you own a freaking mountain."

She laughed softly. "If only I liked baseball, I'd be perfect."

He opened her shirt, revealing a thin silky bra that snapped in the front. "I'll teach you." He unhooked the bra with one click, widening the fabric to expose her breasts.

"And you are perfect," he said huskily, dropping his head to suckle her.

Flames of uncontrolled need licked through her, and she raised her hips to rub against his hard body. His mouth moved over her breasts, laving and kissing and teasing her into a place where want and pain and need and desire all banged together as hard as their bodies did. He kissed his way down her body, caressing her skin with his hot tongue.

Easily, he removed her shirt and bra, leaving her wonderfully bare to the breeze and sun. She tugged at his shirt so he could feel the same way, pulling it over his head, then flipping it onto the grass next to them.

She called out softly as his magnificent bare chest finally touched hers. The course hairs tickled and delighted her supersensitive nipples as they rubbed each other, and their kisses turned frantic.

"Let me," he murmured, unsnapping her pants. "Let me see you. Let me taste you."

The thought liquified her as he slid her zipper down and slipped his hand into her panties. She could only rock against his fingers, a soft groan of pleasure and need escaping her lips. He inched her pants down past her knees, and she kicked off her boots and finished undressing. The grass tickled her thighs, so she lifted her legs and he eased his way down with more hot kisses on her stomach.

He fingered the lace band of her panties. "What do you know? Girl underpants."

She started to laugh, but he placed his mouth over her mound, making the silk as wet on the outside as it was on the inside. With his hands, he spread her thighs and his tongue darted along the edge of the lace, demanding entrance, seeking a way in.

She stabbed her fingers into his golden hair and pushed his head against her, mumbling his name and pleas to stop teasing and taste her.

She could feel him smile, that sexy, lazy, I'm-gonna-get-you grin, and then he moved the silky material to the side, revealing her woman's flesh to him.

He muttered her name softly, then leisurely, deliberately, he stroked her with his tongue.

She thought she'd die. Heat and moisture and pleasure fused between her legs and she lost any control she'd ever had. Digging her hands into his hair, she lifted her hips for more.

He slid her panties down and kissed her stomach, her hip bones, around the side.

"Let me see your pony," he whispered, easing her to her right hip.

Again he kissed her tattoo, tracing the design with his magical tongue.

"Mustang Sally," he whispered against her skin. She closed her eyes, smiling like a fool, blessing Katie for talking her into what seemed like sheer madness at the time.

Then he worked his way around the front and used that sinful, slow, torturous tongue between her legs, darting it around her nub, then sucking her harder and faster and deeper until she heard herself gasp and call his name and shudder in his mouth.

Before she'd recovered, he was kissing his way back up her body, whispering her name, making more promises.

Her fingers started on the clasp of his jeans. "Now me, Cam."

He shook his head. "Baby, I have to be inside you. I have to." He ground the words out as she opened his jeans. "Reach into my back pocket," he instructed.

She did, sliding her hand in and enjoying the sensation of his hard buttocks under her fingertips. Then she felt the foil pack.

"Aren't you the little Boy Scout," she said, surprised.

He laughed softly. "Not little," he promised, taking her hand and guiding it to his shaft.

Pleasure gnawed at him the moment Jo's fingers closed over his flesh. He sucked in a harsh, ragged breath and heard her moan as she slid along the length of his erection. Then she dipped her brilliant, talented fingers into his hot, hard nest and stroked the skin so lightly a grunt of desire caught in his throat.

Using every ounce of willpower not to explode against her, he slid off his jeans and boxers and furiously tore the condom open with his teeth.

The burning need to plunge into her had his whole being throbbing and shaking. She must have recognized that, taking the condom and easing him over on his back.

"Let me," she offered. Again she straddled him, gorgeous and naked with her wild hair tumbling over her shoulders and breasts like some kind of mystical wood nymph he'd found in the mountains.

He gritted his teeth as she loosened the condom, then

slid it down him slowly, torturing him with a tight, demanding squeeze.

She eased herself above him, their gazes locked on each other. He whispered her name, drinking in the sight of her taut, pink nipples and the sweet, sexy mouth he wanted to kiss again. She grabbed his shoulders and squeezed him, her warm, wet opening ready to take him in.

He forced himself to hold back, not to thrust into her. He ripped a handful of grass in his fist as she lowered her face to his.

"You make me feel like such a *girl,*" she whispered, her expression a mix of wonder and delight. "How do you do that?"

"You're kidding, right?" He ran his hands over her hips and buttocks, guiding her onto him, holding her brown-eyed gaze. "You are the most feminine, most beautiful woman I've ever met."

He rolled her over on the grass with one quick movement, positioning himself on top of her. His erection slid right into the wet nest between her legs, causing him to suck in a breath. "Feminine, beautiful and if I don't get inside you, I'm gonna die."

He lifted her hips and plunged into her.

He closed his eyes, lost. Blissfully lost in the mountains, lost in the bone-shattering pleasure of her body.

Rising on his arms, he looked down to the apex where they connected. With each thrust into her, their rhythm increased, their labored breaths grew louder and more ragged. Sweat dripped down his cheeks, and he lowered himself to get that kiss, wanting to be connected on every level, at every point as they reached the end.

She tightened around him, shuddering and exploding against him as her fingers dug into the flesh of his shoulders. Finally the agony and pleasure was too much, wrenching at his groin and squeezing his heart until he finally gave in, kissing her mouth and repeating her name until he'd emptied everything into Jo.

Ten

As he suspected, Cam's cell phone started ringing the minute he'd sent his brothers the e-mail about their mother's will. He'd managed to ignore them for two days. For two incredible, mind-blowing, sensual days, he'd managed to ignore just about everything except the joys of Jo Ellen Tremaine. But he knew he couldn't put the conversation off any longer. Not with his brothers, and not with his lover.

He'd tell her later tonight.

But now...he didn't even look at the Caller ID to know who'd been after him since he'd shared the truth about his mother's last will and testament. It was Quinn or Colin. Or, hell, both.

He grabbed the phone, knowing he had at least ten minutes before Jo returned from the shop. They had one more evening and half day alone in the house, and she'd promised "a surprise." His whole being tightened at the endless possibilities. Another trip up the mountain? Another erotic three-hour bath in that clawfoot tub? And then there was what she'd done with him in the back seat of that Mustang....

He didn't even have a chance to say hello once he hit Talk.

"We're in." Quinn's voice was eerily devoid of his usual lighthearted tone. "Can you bring the baby home now or should we come out there and help you?"

He swallowed hard and resisted the urge to curse. Mightily. "I haven't decided."

"Well, we need to know. Pronto. Nic's out shopping for cribs and stuff. I gotta get airline tickets, and Colin wants to meet us there, too."

A vague sense of disgust rolled through Cam. "I think that's a little premature, bro."

"Premature? You said Mom's will is clear and final." *Mom?* He'd never in his adult life heard Quinn call her *Mom.* "We've talked it to death on this end, and Dad's admitted that her whole story is true. Frankly, it's a big weight off him. He's like a different man."

Cam opened his mouth to speak, but Quinn rattled on. "There's nothing to wait for. The baby is a Mc-Grath. I know Mom's will specified you, but what she wanted was for Callie to be a McGrath. We'll be there Saturday."

"Saturday—?"

"Look, you should know that Colin and Grace want to raise her, too. And if you want to split it three ways, we can do that. I just—"

"Quinn, stop it." Cam clenched his jaw and grabbed hold of his temper, forcing himself to lower his voice. "She's a child, not a...a freakin' pie you can divide! She's a *child.*"

Quinn went silent, leaving Cam with the sounds of cellular static and the pounding of his own pulse.

"I realize that, Cam," his brother finally said. "We just want to do what's right."

"Then stay home."

"What? Have you changed your mind? Now you want to go against what our mother requested? She wanted to be sure Callie is a *McGrath*. Not a…what's that girl's name again?"

His blood turned molten. "Tremaine," he said with all the control he could muster. "Her name is Jo Ellen Tremaine. And she is a beautiful, caring, remarkable woman who will be an outstanding mother to our niece."

"Oh."

Oh? That was definitely not the response Cam had expected. "What do you mean, 'oh'?"

"I mean I hadn't considered you falling in love with her."

"In love?" Cam's back stiffened. "What the hell are you talking about?"

"I thought you were just having fun."

He *was* having fun.

"I know what you're going through, dude," Quinn continued. "It's like one insane, life-threatening roller-coaster ride and you don't know whether it would be more dangerous to jump off and risk death or hang on and lose everything you thought was important."

Cam had to smile. "Somewhere in that brutal mess of metaphors is a pearl of wisdom or two."

"Damn right there is. Hey, I've been there. Don't be afraid to take advice from your little brother."

"I don't need advice," Cam lied. He *did* need advice. Bad.

"So, square with me," Quinn demanded. "How does she make you feel?"

Cam closed his eyes for a second, considering the question. "Healed."

"Oh, yeah?" He heard Quinn's ironic chuckle. "And you were the one who was supposed to heal everyone else's hurt."

"I don't know if it's going to work out that way, bro. Somewhere, somehow, somebody's going to get hurt. Because of me."

"We want Callie, too, Cam. We can love her and take care of her. She belongs with family." There was no indictment in Quinn's voice, no accusation. Just a statement of fact.

"She belongs with Jo. They are an incredible team."

Quinn swore softly under his breath. "Well, then you're right…. Someone's going to get hurt."

Cam heard the truck rumble into the drive and he looked out the window to see Jo in the driver's seat. His stomach dipped…like he *was* on a roller coaster. "Maybe I can figure something out. I need another day." God, he needed more than that. He needed…

He didn't even want to think about how much time he wanted with Jo.

"We're moving ahead with our plans on this end," Quinn said ominously.

Cam hung up without acknowledging the comment, his gaze still locked on Jo as she parked the truck in the driveway.

For a moment she just sat staring straight ahead.

What was she thinking?

And what would she think when he finally told her about his conversation with her mother, about *his* mother's will? He had tried. The words had lodged in his throat a dozen times over the past two days and two nights. But then she'd sensed that something was wrong…and had set to work to fix it.

And, man, the woman could *fix* things.

She fixed him with her incredible hands by massaging his back, washing his hair, touching every cell in his body until he groaned with need and desire and satisfaction. She fixed him with her gentle, sexy mouth, with kisses that melted his brain and whispered words that eased his heart. She fixed him with her humor, generously served up with sarcasm and honesty and interest in his responses.

And, oh God, she fixed him just fine by taking him inside of her, closing her body around his and calling out his name as she rolled like thunder underneath and on top of him.

In his whole life, he couldn't remember feeling so whole and new and repaired. Was that love, as Quinn had pronounced it?

It couldn't be. Because if he loved her, he wouldn't consider shattering her faith in him, and in humanity, by arranging for Callie to go to the McGraths'. The truck door opened, and Cam sucked in a harsh breath at the sight it revealed.

Out slid one long, luscious leg, then another. On her feet were the sexiest pair of black high heels he'd ever seen. His gaze traveled up the endless legs to the short black skirt that hugged her incredible thighs. And farther up to the flimsy white sweater that clung to her perfect breasts. Her hair was loose, over her shoulders. She closed the truck door and walked toward the house like a model on a catwalk, his jaw dropping with each sway of her hips.

Holy tomgirl. She was drop-dead gorgeous.

Speechless, he opened the front door to greet her.

"What's the matter with you, McGrath?" she asked playfully, reaching up to shut his mouth. "Never seen a woman in makeup before?"

"Wow," he managed to say. "I don't know what you have in mind for our date tonight, but maybe I should change."

Her gaze tripped over his pullover polo and khaki pants. "Into what? One of your six-dozen Yankee shirts? You're fine."

He stepped back to let her in, a whiff of something exotic wafting from her. "Where are we going?" Besides paradise.

"That's a surprise," she said as she opened the drawer to an ancient oak dresser near the front door.

"Another surprise?" He continued to rake her with a long, lusty look, lingering on the thigh-high skirt and never-ending legs and do-me-from-the-back shoes. "I thought…the surprise was this outfit."

She casually touched the hem of her skirt, which was *above* her fingertips. "This? Oh, this is just a little something your sister picked out for me." She winked and retrieved a set of jangling keys from the drawer, flipping them to him. "You can drive my Mustang."

"Katie told me these shoes were magic," Jo confided to Cam, sliding one leg sensuously over the other as she shimmied against the cool leather of the Mustang's passenger seat. She loved the feel of the strappy, skimpy high heels, loved the wonderful way her legs tightened when she walked. And, good heavens, she loved the thrill of Cam's long, hungry, appreciative glances.

Oh, yes. She had to do this girly stuff more often.

Cam's gaze swept over her again. "You're magical in them. That's the difference."

"Of course, counselor." She rolled her eyes at his never-ending semantic corrections. "When you get into town, turn left on Carvel and head south."

"Where are we going?"

She glanced at her watch and purposely didn't answer him. "Trust me, you don't want to be late."

Delight trickled through her, giving her the heady sensation of having just one too many cold beers. She'd regret it just like a hangover, too, when he was gone. But, shoot, she didn't feel like fighting this bliss.

He hadn't left, hadn't proved her mother right. Like her father. Like her husband. Cam had traveled across the country, and, so far, he stayed.

So far. And he'd promised she'd have Callie…and he might continue to visit like a good uncle. She'd already decided to tell Callie the truth when she was old enough to understand. No reason to hide her from the McGrath family. Not once Jo had legally adopted her.

No reason at all…except that Jo had a crush on Cam the size of California, and he lived in New York.

She sighed and smoothed the short skirt over her legs. And she'd always have this week. This incredible, memorable week with Cam. And it was just a *crush*.

Wasn't it?

As he drove into town, she felt her body relax and remember every wonderful moment. Since they melted together on the mountain, she'd wallowed in pleasure. Physical, emotional, even, in an odd way, spiritual pleasure. She knew she'd helped him enormously in dealing with his past, and, she realized that afternoon when she'd changed at the shop and thought about Katie, she'd been helped, too.

"I know you think I was jealous of her," she said softly, surprising herself with the admission. "And in a way I always was."

"Jealous? Of Katie?" He glanced at her. "I wouldn't characterize it as jealousy. More like sibling rivalry. I'm very familiar with that."

"She *was* like my sister," Jo agreed, looking out the window and seeing Katie's wickedly cute grin and her sparkling brown eyes. "It just seemed like I spent a good deal of my life getting her out of trouble. And then in the end…" She closed her eyes.

"You couldn't get her out of the worst trouble of all." He closed his hand over her leg. "And you haven't accepted that. In fact, you're still mad at her for dying without giving you a chance to save her."

She turned away from the window to look at him in disbelief. "Well, who's turned into the shrink now?"

He squeezed her hand. "Hey. People change. And grow. And learn from each other."

She wondered if he could hear her heart flipping and landing low in her stomach at that comment. "That's right, Cam," she responded, pointing toward a flashing yellow sign at the entrance to The Sports Section. "And to prove that point, please pull in there."

"There? What is there?"

"A bar."

He threw her a confused glance. "A sports bar?"

"Yep." She tapped the face of her watch. "And the first pitch is in five minutes. So you better hustle if you don't want to miss Mussina's slider. I heard it's…" she lowered her voice and copped a fake "New Yawk" accent, "Friggin' magical."

His eyes opened wide and his grin could melt the snow on Mount Shasta. "They get the game here?"

"The boys in pinstripes are playing the A's tonight." She pointed to the old Sierra Springs institution, known locally as The Section. "And you can see it on satellite, right here in the house that *somebody*—but not Babe Ruth—built in 1976."

He pulled her face to his and kissed her so hard he had to have devoured all the lip gloss she'd brushed on with the same amount of care she'd give a hairline metal fracture.

"Quinn's right," he said as he broke the kiss. "I am in love with you."

Before she could open her eyes, he'd jumped out of the car and was winging around to her side to get the door.

He was in *love* with her?

Her heart thumped wildly as she heard the words replay over and over in her head. *In love with her?*

And then her heart tripped at the next thought. *Why* had he been talking to his brother?

Cam never mentioned love—or Quinn—for the next several hours. Jo tried hard to forget the comment and forced herself to get lost in the game and enjoy Cam's enthusiasm for the victory his team enjoyed that night. They drank a few beers, ate burgers, cheered loudly and celebrated every good play with a kiss.

Nothing was different.

Except that Cam had said he was in love with her.

Good God, now what?

When he pulled the Mustang into the garage, Cam turned to her with what could only be described as an evil, lascivious, delicious look in his eyes.

"I love that you took me to watch the game," he said. Love again. Uh-oh. "And I love what you wore," he added, running a single finger over her leg until it settled on the inside of her thigh. "And I'm going to love to watch it all come off tonight."

She could barely swallow as the familiar heat started to boil under her flesh, the wonderful tightness pulled her stomach and the melting started between her legs. "All of it?" she managed to ask.

"Keep the shoes on."

She threw her head back and laughed, but he caught her in another mouthwatering kiss.

"Come on, tomgirl," he whispered, fluttering warm kisses down her throat and gliding his hands over her breasts. "Let's go to bed."

"Bed?" she teased. "You're so pedestrian tonight."

He shook his head as his hand dipped into her cleavage and his fingers found her hardened nipple. "Not pedestrian. Traditional. I'm in the mood for traditional."

"With my heels on."

"Traditional with a twist."

He kept her laughing and kissing and caressing all the way upstairs. Enough so that she didn't think about those words he'd spoken earlier.

Not love. No, not *love*. *Lust* was okay. *Like* was even acceptable, since they'd always have Callie to keep them connected.

But love? If she let herself love him, how could she stand it when he got on that plane and left her? When he returned to his metal monolith and important job? She'd ache for him.

Ignoring the warning bells, she let him guide her into her darkened bedroom, then he snapped on the tiny night lamp on the dresser. The soft light seeped into the dark corners and washed the room in a low golden glow. She lightly nudged him onto the foot of the bed and stood in front of him as he sat staring at her.

She stepped back, out of his reach, but not out of his sight.

Wordlessly, to a silent beat she heard in her head, she began to strip.

His jaw slackened and his gaze dropped.

She tugged the white sweater out of the waistband of the skirt and slowly pulled it over her head. When it was off, she dropped it on the floor and shook her head, letting her long hair fall around her shoulders.

Then she touched the front clasp of her bra with one finger, moistening her lips with her tongue.

His eyes widened. "You—" he mouthed the word and pointed to her "—are one sexy woman." A wild sensation jumped through her. Power. Danger. Sex.

Yeah. This was *fun*.

And if this was what it felt like to be a girly-girl, a feminine, daring, provocative woman, then she was in for life. She managed not to smile with the sheer joy of her discovery, as she removed her bra and exposed her breasts to him.

He drank her in, the unbridled lust in his eyes zinging her nipples to attention. She slid the skirt over her hips, and as she did, driven by some female fox she didn't even know lived inside of her, she turned around and slowly bent over. Just enough to hear him moan. Just enough to show off her black thong and high heels.

And tattoo.

"Now that's what I call a twist on traditional." His voice was husky. "And don't even think about taking those shoes off."

She ran her hands slowly up her legs until she stood straight, then slowly turned back to him, tweaking her peaked breasts with her fingertips. Taking two slow steps toward him, she reached her arms around his neck and lifted her chest to him with an invitation in her eyes.

She heard him swear softly under his breath, then his mouth closed over one breast, his hand over the other. His lips were like fire on her skin, and she dug her fingers into his hair and pressed against him.

She kissed the top of his head, bursting with the need to share her newfound feminine thrill with him. "Cam," she whispered, pulling his face up to hers. "I have to tell you something."

He released her and looked up into her eyes. "What is it, Jo? What do you want to tell me?"

He looked so expectant. Like he knew what she was going to say. How could he? "I'm not a tomboy after all."

He dropped his head back and let out a quick laugh. "What was your first clue?"

"Seriously," she told him, easing him on his back. "I never thought I could pull off this sexy, girly stuff. You know. I'm a collision-repair expert."

"I know you are." His voice had turned serious and low. "You sure fixed me."

The look in his eyes took her breath away. "I did?"

He nodded, pulling her gently on top of him. "I've never felt so together, so whole in my life, Jo. All that old stuff—" he shook his head in wonder "—that pain is gone."

His words were like music to her heart. Tracing his cheek and jaw with a single finger, she whispered, "I told you wrecks were my specialty."

He glided his hands over her back, his fingers closing around the strap of her thong. "You're very, very good, Jo Tremaine."

With a sly smile, she leaned up on her hands. "I'm not done yet."

Slowly she unbuckled his belt, unfastened his pants and pushed them down. He helped her with his shoes and boxers, then pulled his shirt over his head.

"Let me do this," she whispered. "Let me."

"No objections, honey." She laughed a little at his lawyerly tone, then began to flutter kisses over the course hair of his muscular chest. She licked her way down each stomach muscle—one, two, three beautiful planes of manliness—and then enclosed him in her two hands.

"Oh…" He groaned softly and moved into her hands.

Her tongue darted over the velvety head, tasting salt and skin and the delicious essence of Cameron's moisture. Slowly she eased him into her mouth, as a rumble started somewhere deep in his chest and his fingers tightened his grip on her hair.

That same insane sense of power and femininity rolled through her, twisting her own core with desire, thrilling her.

She buried him against her tongue and teeth, and over the thumping of her pulse she heard him say her name and plead for more.

She quieted him with one hand flat on his stomach and the other curled around him. Her tongue encircled him, her lips pulled just enough to torture and tease him and her fingers nestled into the warm sack of his manhood.

She consumed him as far as she could with her mouth, her hand stroking the rest of him. Suddenly his grip on her shoulders tightened.

"Wait." Did he say *wait?* "C'mere," he urged, reaching under her arms to pull her up.

"I'm busy." She tried to sound put out, but he wasn't kidding. His expression was solemn, his eyes dark with unsaid words as they searched her face. "What is it, Cam?"

He just shook his head for a second, as though he

couldn't talk. "I want to make love to you," he finally whispered.

"Isn't that what we're doing?"

He almost smiled. "You're giving me pleasure."

"That's the general idea, counselor. Do you have to clarify every point?"

"I want to make *love* to you." This time he said it very slowly, as though English were not her first language. "I want to show you that I..." His words faltered, his eyes narrowed.

And her heart stopped.

Before he could say it, she kissed him, rubbing herself over his erection and hopefully stopping him from saying what she was terrified to hear.

If he loved her, it would hurt far too much if...if he left.

Reaching over to the nightstand, she grabbed one of the few condoms they had left. "Okay," she agreed. "You win."

Tearing it open with her teeth and keeping her gaze trained on him, she pulled out the flattened disk of latex with trembling hands and slid it over him with expert speed. Still on top of him, she sat up and lowered herself onto him, dropping her head back as he entered her.

Her hair tickled her lower back, and Cameron's fingers twined into it. She expected him to grab her hips, to furiously move her over him.

But he was changing the rules. He had the hungry look of desire, but he pulled her body down so that their chests touched and he kissed her.

"Take it easy, sweetheart," he crooned into a kiss. "Easy."

As if to demonstrate, he matched each leisurely thrust of his tongue with an equally measured thrust of his body into her. He gently rocked against her, then stopped, pressing her so tightly against him, so deeply inside her that she could feel the tip of him touch the farthest reaches of her body.

"Jo Ellen," he whispered against her mouth. "Listen to me."

She closed her eyes and held on. "Yes?"

"I love you."

She heard the whimper that came from her throat. Cam, don't do this. Don't make this hurt when it's over.

But she couldn't say anything. Instead she lunged harder over him. He squeezed her hips. "Did you hear me?" he demanded gently.

She just writhed up and down, letting the incredible feeling erase everything. All common sense. All potential loss and pain. Everything but the burning need to keep moving until she lost herself and let the words and the erotic sensations collide inside of her.

It started quickly. A tight coil inside her, wrapped around his erection. She clutched his hips with her legs. He loosened his grip and let her ride. Faster. Harder. She sheathed herself over him, feeling him all the way inside her.

She squeezed her eyes closed and heard her own short, ragged breath, heard her voice moan and say his name.

And she heard him repeat those deadly words. "I love you," he whispered to her. "I love you, Jo."

The pressure was too much. She bucked against him as her whole body constricted around his, and then waves of heavenly relief rocked her and rocked her and rocked her until she was lost in a haze of satisfaction.

At that moment he thrust one last, furious time into her, and a long, agonizing moan tore from his chest as he climaxed.

Sweat mixed with tears and saliva on her cheeks, so

she buried her face into his neck and listened to the words that pounded in her brain. *I love you, too.*

But she refused to say them out loud.

Eleven

He could no longer postpone the inevitable heartbreak of the truth. The right thing to do. The healing of the Mc-Grath hurt, no matter how much it hurt her.

Was it possible she would understand? Could they find a compromise? A way she could stay in Callie's life but have his mother's and his brother's wishes fulfilled?

He waited until both of their breathing had slowed, until their mingled perspiration had left them chilled.

He started by pulling her into his chest, close to his heart. "Jo, I need to tell you something."

"I don't want to talk," she said sleepily, sitting up to unbuckle the shoes she still wore. "I need to get under the covers. I'm cold. I'm tired."

While she sat on the edge of the bed and removed the last vestiges of her sex-kitten act, he straightened the comforter and waited for her to join him.

Turning on his side, he studied her stiff movements

in the lamplight. He recognized an uncooperative witness when he faced one. "I want to ask you a question."

"I sense a cross-examination, counselor."

He laughed at how well she knew him already, but continued. "Do you believe me?"

They both knew that he referred to his admission of love. She waited a moment before answering.

"Here's what I think," she finally said. "I think you're floating in an unreal state of euphoria because you have finally rid yourself of the biggest heartache in your life. And you think I'm responsible for this newfound joy. But all I did was tell you—"

He sat up and touched her arm. "All you did was drop into my life and force me to grow up and feel things that have petrified me for years."

She turned to him, her eyes wide and sincere. "Are you petrified of love?"

He nodded. "I was."

"Well, I still *am*."

At the catch in her throat, he pulled her into his arms and laid her next to him. She'd told him of her first husband leaving. He knew about her father taking off when she was a baby. No wonder she was scared.

But, damn, if he didn't tell her now about his mother's will, he could rightfully be accused of being the most deceptive, immoral man in the world, raising her distrust of men to a new level altogether.

He took a deep breath. "I have to tell you something that I think is going to upset you."

"You already have." Her lips kicked into a droll smile.

"My mother left a will."

He felt her whole body stiffen.

"She stipulated that if she should be…incapacitated

in any way during a time when she was in custody of Callie, that said custody should revert to me." He swallowed, hating the lawyerly tone that had taken over.

Slowly she lifted herself to a half-sitting position. "Excuse me?"

"Your mother showed me the will."

She blinked at him. "What are you saying? What difference does it make? They are both dead."

"My mother lived for hours after Katie died, Jo." He forced his voice to be gentle. "Technically, what she foresaw actually happened."

"She said that because Katie was a flight risk!" Jo practically shouted. "She was immature and given to stupid decisions. She thought Katie might leave town, if the pressure of being a mom was too much, and she was worried about the baby. Not because she thought…she thought—oh!" She dropped her head into her hands and let out a low moan. "Even she didn't think I was a suitable mother."

"What?" He sat up and took her shoulders. "What are you talking about?"

"They always joked about it. They teased me about being a tomboy, about not having maternal instincts, about holding a man's job." She blew out a frustrated breath. "Deep inside, Aunt Chris didn't even think I could be Callie's mother."

"No, no," he insisted, trying to fold her into him. "She thought Callie would bring our family back together. To finally close wounds that my dad created through sheer stupidity and stubbornness."

Her eyes flashed in the dim light. "Do you believe that? For one second, do you really believe that?"

"I don't know what I believe anymore," he admitted.

"I just know that…" He took another long, slow breath. "My brothers are coming here on Saturday to get Callie."

She jumped out of his arms, the raw, real pain on her face visible even in the dim light.

"But I don't agree with that, Jo, and I—"

In a flash she was off the bed. "Stop talking, Cam. Just don't say another word."

She bounded to her closet, yanked open the door and pulled on jeans and a T-shirt. Slowly he started to climb from the bed, but she twirled around and held out one hand.

"Stop. Don't move. Don't talk."

He froze and watched her slide into little brown boots. Then she stared at him.

This was his sentencing. This was his punishment. Would she ever give him a chance? All he wanted to do was work this out. Be with her.

Marry her and raise Callie together.

The realization almost knocked him over. God in heaven, that was what he wanted. He started to speak, to tell her, to *propose* to her, but then she held both hands up.

"I'm leaving now. When I come back, you'll be gone. Do you understand?" Her voice didn't so much as quiver.

He just looked at her. If he asked her to marry him now, she'd laugh in his face. No matter how much he meant it. And he did. He would leave New York in a heartbeat. He wasn't happy at his job anymore. He'd take the California Bar. Live here, in the mountains, with Jo and Callie and—

"Do you understand?" she repeated. "I want you to be gone by morning when I come home with Callie."

"Jo. Listen to me. I'm serious—"

"Gone." He could see her clench her jaw as she raised

her face to him. "And don't you ever throw around the word *love* in front of me again."

Without another word she walked out of the room and clunked down the creaky steps in her boy boots. He heard the truck start up and the gravel spew as she drove into the night.

Before he packed his bag, he wrote one long, honest e-mail to Colin and Quinn and hoped they read it before they went to sleep that night. They needed to know where he stood.

The first thing Jo intended to do when she arrived at her mother's house was wake up Callie.

"What are you doing, Jo?" Her mother was hot on her heels as they traveled down the hallway, her tone revealing that she was none too happy with her daughter's near-midnight arrival, and doubly unhappy about waking the baby. "I just gave her a bottle an hour ago. Don't you dare wake up that child."

But Jo ignored her mother and dipped into the portable crib she kept in Jo's childhood bedroom of the tiny ranch house. Callie stirred and gurgled, then snuggled into Jo's arm.

"Hey, peanut, I missed you," Jo whispered, kissing the black curls and closing her eyes to inhale the scent she loved. "I really missed you."

Her mother leaned against the doorjamb, and Jo shot her a long, angry look. She was as much a part of this conspiracy as Aunt Chris and her masters-of-the-universe sons.

But first, all Jo wanted to do was suck in a deep breath of Callie. She dropped onto the twin bed where she'd slept as a little girl, and cuddled the baby closer. Then she looked up at her mother.

"They're taking her."

Alice nodded slowly. "I thought they might."

Jo felt her eyes narrow in fury. "Why would you do this to me? To Callie?"

Shaking her head slowly, Alice stepped into the room. "Baby, I'm not doing anything to you."

When she sat on the bed, Jo instinctively turned the baby away and her mother's eyes darkened with hurt.

"You're not? You didn't even *tell* me about this will. You told him." She shook her head. "You told him first."

And the next thing he did was make love to her on the mountainside, she realized with a jolt of anger and indignation.

Alice sighed deeply. "Honey, that's what Aunt Chris wanted. And you have to understand something. For the last twenty-six years, I've carried the burden of Chris McGrath's secret. All she wanted in the whole world was for her daughter to know her sons. But she was so scared those boys had developed such a hatred for her, that they would shun Katie. So she waited and waited."

"She waited too long," Jo said softly. "Anyway, she was dead wrong. They would have loved Katie as much as we did." Cameron would have, anyway, and she suspected the other two were made of the same stuff. Fair. Good. Kind.

Her heart squeezed, and she tugged Callie a little tighter into her chest.

"Yes, she did wait too long," her mother agreed, reaching over to touch Callie's little head. "But I owed her closure and peace. She was my closest friend. My dearest, dearest friend. She came to my rescue as much as I came to hers all those years ago. I was still smarting from your father walking out, wondering how on earth I would raise a child alone. And she swooped into

Sierra Springs and we were unified. A better friend never existed."

Jo shifted to look at her mother. "That's fine, Mom. I respect that. But do you really think she belongs with the McGraths and not us?"

Alice drew in a long, deep breath, her gaze moving from the baby to Jo. "Chris obviously believed she belongs with blood. That family has been ripped in half, and it appears those boys are just coming out of years of pain. And finding happiness, from what your Cameron told me the other day."

"He's not *my* Cameron," she corrected. "But what about Katie? She was Callie's mother. Would she have wanted her baby to be raised by strangers, even strangers whose blood she unknowingly shared?"

"That's a good point," Alice acknowledged. "But you know what Katie was like. Always searching for that man to be the father she never had. I suspect finding out she had three big brothers who could love her might have made her happier than any of the short flings she indulged in over the years."

Jo silently agreed. Katie would have adored Cameron. And he, she knew, would have been just as charmed by Katie. He might have finally set her on the straight path—one that Jo had tried, but failed, to show Katie.

A hard, painful lump formed in her throat, and she attempted to get rid of it by kissing Callie.

Maybe she wasn't cut out to be a mother. Or a girly-girl.

Just a tomboy collision-repair expert.

And maybe Callie's destiny was more closely tied to the McGrath family than Jo was willing to admit.

A tear slid down her cheek and landed on Callie's forehead.

The baby stirred as Jo dabbed the moisture gently and Callie opened her eyes. For a moment they stared at each other. Then Callie smiled and reached a dimpled hand to Jo's nose.

"Jojojojojo."

Jo closed her eyes and lifted Callie into her chest, burying her little face with kisses.

"I'm going to lose everything," she whispered to her mother, the tears flowing freely now. "I've lost Katie. And I lost Cam. And now I'm going to lose Callie."

Her mother wrapped an arm around Jo's shoulder. "They won't keep you out of her life, honey. You can visit her and write to her and always be her aunt Jo."

But she didn't want to be Callie's aunt Jo.

She wanted to be Callie's mother.

"She lived for a reason, Mom." Jo looked hard at her mother. "She has a destiny."

Alice nodded slowly. "Yes, she does. And you know what that is."

Yes, Jo thought quietly, yes. She did know what Callie's destiny was. And she just couldn't fight it anymore.

"You brought the baby?" Mary Beth Borrell raised both eyebrows, her sharp features easily communicating her displeasure. "There was no reason to bring the child."

Defiantly Jo hoisted Callie a bit higher in her arms and met the green-eyed glare of the Child Services social worker she'd come to know all too well over the past three months.

"Yes, I did," she said, walking to the single guest chair in Mary Beth's tiny office. "We won't be long today, Mary Beth, and I thought I'd take Callie for new shoes while we're in Sacramento." A whole new wardrobe, actually. That she could wear in Florida. Or Rhode Island. Or New York.

"Don't sit down." Mary Beth stopped her with another sharp look. "We're all in the conference room."

Jo's heart dipped. All? Had Cam come after all? Didn't he trust her to come forward with the truth?

Mary Beth indicated for Jo to follow her into the narrow hallway of the old government building, their heels tapping on the buckled linoleum floor. Just before they reached a single door with a milky glass panel, Mary Beth turned, her displeasure having morphed to something akin to disgust.

"I wish you'd told me sooner," she said. "I trusted you from the beginning of this."

Jo backed up an inch and felt the blood drain from her head. So Cam was in that room. He really *didn't* trust her.

"I only recently learned about the family," Jo said quietly. "And I have all the necessary paperwork to arrange for him to have custody of Callie."

Mary Beth frowned, confusion darkening her green eyes. "We don't need these kinds of complications, Ms. Tremaine."

"No." Jo tried to keep the sarcasm out of her voice. "We certainly don't, Ms. Borrell."

"I thought this was a cut-and-dried case."

Callie turned in Jo's arms and looked at the other woman, somehow sensing the hostility between them. Grab her nose, Cal, Jo thought. Go ahead.

But the baby dropped her head on Jo's shoulder in an uncharacteristic bout of shyness.

Mary Beth's face softened. "We can handle it," she said quickly as she turned the doorknob. "I was just a bit overwhelmed by the three of them."

The *three* of them? Jo barely took a breath before the

door opened to reveal three striking, large, handsome men sitting side by side at a conference room table.

They stood in unison, like a six-foot-two wall of masculinity, and she could practically feel the balance of power slide to that side of the room.

As if she ever had a chance against these guys.

Forcing herself to focus, she looked at the man in front of her. Tall, with the lanky build of an athlete, he had close-cropped dark hair except for one loose lock over his handsome brow. His lip curled in a half smile as his gaze dropped just far enough over her face to feel completely checked out.

Quinn, the ladies' man.

He confirmed it by reaching out his hand and introducing himself. She shifted Callie into her left arm and shook his hand. "Hello, Quinn."

She looked to his left and met the dark-chocolate gaze of Colin McGrath. His grin was warm and immediate, and he tilted his head as he reached out his hand. She noticed a tiny gold earring and a ponytail, but her focus was on those eyes. That smile. For a second she was so overwhelmed with the loss of Katie, she couldn't speak. They really could have been twins.

Colin, the rebel.

"I'm Colin," he said, his expression as warm as his handshake. "And this must be Callie."

She shifted Callie in her arms so they could see her. "Yes. This is your niece."

Both men's faces brightened as they focused on the baby, but Jo just froze. She had to face Cam. He stood next to Colin, and she could feel his gaze on her.

Would he be cold? Mean? Call her *Ms. Tremaine* as if they hadn't shared hours of ecstasy and days of... love?

Finally she looked up at him. "Hi, Cam."

"Jo Ellen." His voice was low, his expression tender.

She swallowed and managed a weak smile, but his gaze moved to Callie.

"Hi-ya, kid." He grinned at the baby, who beamed right back at him.

"Cacacaca!" She held both arms out to him.

Cam laughed and reached for her, and Jo didn't even fight it. She hoisted the baby over the table and gave Cam a look of pure defeat. Callie cooed with delight when he took her.

Even Callie knew where she really belonged.

"Well, now." Mary Beth noisily scraped out the chair at the head of the table and took her seat, nodding to everyone to do the same. "It seems our little Callie has family after all." Her stern gaze moved to Cameron. "Or so they say."

Jo sat up at the comment and looked at Mary Beth. "They are telling the truth. These men are Callie's blood uncles. I have everything you need to see to prove it."

Callie's pudgy hands curled around Cam's index fingers, and she stood her little legs on his lap, doing her march as if to prove that someday, very soon, she could actually walk like all these other people.

Colin cracked up and glanced at Quinn, who stared at the baby like he'd never seen anything so adorable in his whole life.

A strange flood of relief washed through Jo. This would be fine. This would be *fine*.

Most important, this would be right.

She leaned forward and looked hard at Mary Beth. "Obviously, I was premature in seeking custody and starting the adoption process of Callie McGrath." She willed her voice to be steady and strong, aware of Cam's unwavering gaze on her. She didn't meet it. "After a great deal of consideration, I have elected to drop those efforts and will move forward at the court's direction to arrange for a representative from the McGrath family to adopt Callie."

The room went silent. Mary Beth's jaw fell open. The stunned looks of the McGrath brothers burned her.

"What?" Cam finally broke the tension and set Callie on the table, holding her tiny waist with his massive hands.

"I'm not going to fight you, Cam," she said softly. Her gaze traveled to Colin, then to Quinn. "Callie should be raised with…family." She praised her inner strength for being able to say that without her voice cracking.

That must be because she finally believed it.

"Well, this is highly unusual." Mary Beth's voice rose at least an octave. "I'm not sure we've ever had a case quite like this before. I may have to get a supervisor in here."

"Why?" Jo asked. "There's plenty of precedent." She glanced at Cam. "Ask the lawyer."

But Cam's eyes had turned an intense shade of blue. "We've already signed the petition, Jo. She's yours. We're not taking her."

All her inner strength melted like powdery spring snow at his words. "Are you serious?"

He nodded, punctuating the confirmation with a kiss on Callie's forehead. "We decided she needs to stay with you. You've been a mother to her, Jo. I can't…" He exchanged a meaningful glance with his brothers, and when he looked back at her, she saw a lifetime of pain in his eyes. "We can't be responsible for separating a child from its mother."

The unfamiliar burn of tears stung her eyelids. If she so much as blinked, the waterworks would fall. She swallowed again, hoping her voice would be there when she needed it.

Quinn leaned forward, reaching across the table and putting his hand over hers. "We've agreed on this, Jo. Cam convinced us it's the right way to proceed."

She looked up at him and tried to smile. Damn the tears. All she could do was nod.

"We'd love it if you brought her back east once in a while," Colin added with a devilish grin. "So we can spoil her rotten."

That did it. She blinked. Great. The one time in her life she needed to act like a tomboy and she turned into a virtual crybaby.

She took a deep breath and looked from one McGrath to the other. "Katie would have—" her voice caught and she sniffed a little "—Katie would have loved you all."

Colin's eyes glimmered and Quinn smiled sadly. She stole a look at Cameron, who just warmed her with an expression she recognized as well as her own face. The look he gave her after they made love. Or when she made him laugh. That look of admiration and respect and…love.

She sternly reminded herself that he credited her with some miraculous healing of his heart. Not love. Not real love, anyway. She had to remember that, because it would make saying goodbye easier.

"I promise that you'll know her, and see her," she told them. "I promise that she'll always be part of your family."

Mary Beth stood up. "All righty, then. We'll proceed with the formal adoption of Callie McGrath by Jo Ellen Tremaine. Thank you."

As soon as Mary Beth left the room, Colin and Quinn descended on Callie, making silly sounds and jokes and vying for her attention. And just like her mother, Callie treated them to a megawatt smile that elicited a round of appreciative laughter.

Cameron handed the baby to Quinn. "Better practice, bro. I'll be right back."

Quinn responded with a questioning look. "Where are you going?"

"To jump off a roller coaster," he said, and they shared a knowing look.

"Good luck," Quinn replied, taking the baby.

"It's a good ride," Colin added.

A roller coaster? Jo ignored the inside joke, slowly standing on legs that threatened to buckle from the wild happiness that danced through her. She was *keeping* Callie. Forever.

She reached for the Winnie-the-Pooh diaper bag on the floor, and when she straightened, Cam was inches from her.

"Can I talk to you for a minute?" he asked, his voice low with solemnity.

She tilted her head toward the hallway where they could talk. Of course she had to thank him. She had to apologize for the way she acted the other night.

As she turned, she noticed Colin and Quinn grinning at each other. More inside jokes. She might not get the joke, but she understood what Cam wanted. A more pleasant, civil goodbye.

Because their goodbye had always been inevitable.

Twelve

"There's probably a better way to do this, Jo," Cam said as they stepped into the hall.

"I know. I know there is," she agreed.

She did?

Before he could continue, she put her hand on his arm and gave him a gentle squeeze. "Thank you, Cam. I can't tell you how much I appreciate what you've done."

Even in the fluorescent lights of a decrepit old county building, Jo's eyes had a golden sparkle to them. Of course, that might have been caused by the tears.

He'd never seen her cry before today, he realized. She'd been ready to give up Callie. For him. The urge to pull her into his arms and kiss her shook him to the bones. But he controlled it. "So, were you really ready to surrender or was that a bluff?"

She bit back a laugh. "No, it wasn't a bluff. I'd given it a lot of thought. I talked to my mother for a long time.

Believe me, I didn't—I *don't*—want to lose Callie. But I wouldn't fight you for her." She bit her lower lip and let out a slow breath. "But this is so much better. Please, please tell your brothers that I appreciate them coming out here. I'm sure it went a long way to assuring Mary Beth that you were serious."

He started to speak, but she tightened her grip on his arm and interrupted him. "I also want to say that I'm sorry about how mad I got at you the other night."

"Don't worry about that," he said, still fighting the urge to kiss her. "I understand your reaction. It was perfectly reasonable."

Her lips curled up in a half smile. "Not exactly reasonable, but thank you. And I promise to…to…" She looked away as though she were gathering her forces again, then met his gaze. "Stay in touch."

His heart sank an inch or two.

"Stay in touch?" He frowned at her. Was his vision of their future that different from hers?

"Well…" Her tight smile discouraged him even further. "There's always e-mail. And you can stop by sometime."

Stop by? "Yeah, anytime I just happen by the Sierra Nevadas."

"You know what I mean."

"I do. And I don't like it."

A little V formed between her eyes as she frowned. "What do you mean?"

"I want more."

She didn't say anything for a long moment. "More?"

He leaned forward, lifting her chin closer to his face. "I want it all."

"All?" He could have sworn her voice cracked again. Would she cry when he asked her to marry him? He hoped the proposal would mean that much to her. Hoped it would fill her with the same overwhelming joy he'd seen in her face a few minutes earlier.

He couldn't wait to find out. "I want to spend my life with you."

If he hadn't been holding her little chin, it would have hit the ground. "Life?"

"You know. Mornings. Afternoons. Nights and weekends. You've heard of life."

"Why?"

Well, that was definitely not the resounding response he'd been hoping for. "Because I love you."

She gave her head a sharp shake. "No, you don't."

"Yes. I do."

"You think you do." She backed up a step and pointed one finger at him. "But you're just…grateful for everything that's happened the past few weeks. This isn't love."

"Easy, Dr. Freud."

"And anyway, I'm not going to New York—"

"I want to live here."

Her eyes popped open like shiny new pennies. "Here? In Sierra Springs?"

"I like it," he said, hating that her reaction wasn't accompanied with quite the choir of angels he'd hoped for. "I can take the California Bar. I really want to practice law again, not manage other people who do. I thought I could—"

She held up her "stop everything" hand. "You don't know what you're saying, Cam. In a few weeks you'll get sick of it. Sick of the small town and the lack of…of…*Yankees*. You'll hate it, then you'll hate me."

Was she serious? "I don't care about the Yankees." Now if that wasn't a declaration of love, what was?

"No," she said simply. "You'll leave."

"I will not," he declared.

But she just looked at him and gave her head another tiny shake. "You won't stay," she said softly. "I know that."

He felt his short glimmer of happiness slip away as he tried to psych her out. He'd have to convince her he was different from the other men who'd broken her heart.

"Jo, I won't leave you," he said quietly. "I wouldn't stand here and ask you to marry me if I—"

"Marry?"

"Well, yeah." Jeez, this was a freaking disaster. "What did you think? I just want to live with you? I told you, I lo—"

She put her hand over his mouth, her eyes wild now. "Please don't, Cam. I can't stand it. I just can't take it."

Slowly he removed her hand from his mouth and threaded his fingers through hers. "Do you love me?"

She just stared at him, saying nothing. Nothing.

He wondered if she could actually hear the sound of his heart breaking as each second ticked by. Finally he asked, "Could you love me, Jo?"

"I could never take that risk." The resolve in her voice was all it took to stop him.

He dropped her hand. He wasn't going to beg. He wasn't prepared to make a closing argument. He'd lost this one.

The sudden outburst of men's laughter broke their moment. He leaned close to her ear, taking that last whiff of her beautiful lemony scent, that last tickle of her hair on his lips.

"You're quite a woman, tomgirl," he whispered. "I'll never forget you."

She looked up and rewarded him with a tearful smile.

Callie's cry woke Jo from a light sleep. Throwing back the sheet, Jo welcomed the cool mountain air on her bare skin. July in the Sierras was the best month for sleeping in the buff.

"I'm coming, sweetie," she called out as she reached for the T-shirt she'd been wearing before bed, and slid on her Sponge Bob boxers.

Somehow, this middle-of-the-night ritual had become part of their routine. Without a doubt, every parenting book ever written would frown mightily on the big, bad habit they'd developed in the past month, but Jo had stopped worrying about the experts around the third night.

It was too good. Too wonderful. The secret hour she spent with Callie. And Cam.

Callie was standing in her crib, crying softly when Jo slipped into the room.

"Hey, lollipop, why ya cryin'?"

"Jojojojojojo!"

"That's what they call me." Jo reached into the crib and glanced at the Piglet and Tigger clock on the wall. Twelve forty-five. Just before ten on the East Coast. "Good timing, my love. Let's get our drinks."

She tiptoed down the stairs with Callie in her arms, out of habit inching to the side that didn't creak.

How had this happened? Oh, she knew exactly how it happened. By accident the first time. By design the second time. Then by silent, mutual agreement.

In the kitchen she popped an already-poured bottle in the microwave, hit the appropriate buttons and then untwisted the cap to her beer.

"We are bad, bad girls," she whispered to Callie.

"Ba-ba!" Callie reached toward the beer bottle, but Jo pulled it away.

"Not *that* bad, dollface." The microwave beeped and Jo shook the bottle to cool it off before handing it to Callie. "This ba's for you."

Five minutes later, Jo was logged on. A few seconds after that, the instant-message notification dinged and the familiar blue-and-white NY logo popped up. Yank-fan002 sending an instant message.

How are my beautiful girls?

It was always his first question.

For some reason that she'd stopped trying to figure out, her eyes teared, as they usually did, as she adjusted Callie on her lap and started typing with one hand.

"We're his girls," she whispered to Callie. "His beautiful girls. And don't we love that?"

An hour later Callie had crashed, Jo's beer was warm, and the final cyber goodbyes had been exchanged. Upstairs, Jo changed Callie and put her down, then stripped off her T-shirt and shorts and slithered over her cool sheets, remembering the nights Cam had been with her.

For nearly five weeks, not a day had gone by without him contacting her. If they didn't communicate on the computer, he called her at work. Or in the evenings, after she'd put Callie to bed and he sat in his magnificent office watching the sun set over Manhattan.

With every conversation, they'd gotten closer. He'd never again said a word about marriage, moving to California, or "life." And Jo knew he never would. It would have to be on her terms, if those words were ever spoken again.

She closed her eyes and replayed their electronic conversation. Just basic stuff. About work. Callie. His brothers. The games he'd be attending this coming weekend.

A strange, deep ache filled her body. It had taken all these extra weeks, and a clear head with the adoption issue behind them, but now Jo could see what Cam already knew when he asked her to marry him.

He could be trusted. He would stay. She believed that

now. But would he ever give her a second chance? Would he ever walk into her shop, or knock on her door…and ask again?

No, she somehow doubted he would ever make himself that vulnerable again. If the words were spoken, they'd be spoken by her, and they'd have to be on his turf.

She closed her eyes and dreamed of Cam…on his turf.

Cam gave the stadium security guard an easy knuckle tap. "'S'up, Ed."

"Dude, you flyin' solo again tonight?"

Cam held up his two tickets and waved them toward his box seats. "You wanna sit with me, Eddie?"

"Don't I wish," Eddie said, making a pretend grab for the ticket but purposely missing it. "Hey, Cam, whatever happened to that California chick with the ten-gallon hat? She was hot, man."

"She dumped me."

He looked dumbstruck. "You're sh—kiddin' me. She dumped a good-looking rich guy like you? Whadya think o' that?"

He tried *not* to think of that. But he just gave Eddie a cocky grin. "She told you she didn't like baseball."

"Guess she wasn't kidding," Eddie said, then punched Cam's arm lightly. "Hey, you're better off without a chick who don't wanna to watch ball. Who needs that?"

He did. "I don't seem to have much of a choice."

Eddie shook his head at the injustices in the world, while Cam took his seat and greeted some familiar faces. By the time they finished the "Star Spangled Banner," he had a beer, peanuts and one empty seat next to him.

His eyes scanned the stands. He studied the couples. The little kids. Familiar faces and strangers.

Had he always felt this alone in Yankee Stadium?

Only after Jo. Before that, he was too wounded, blind and stubborn to know better. But now he was healed. And smart. And…still stubborn.

No. He wasn't stubborn. He was just biding his time. A few more months of e-mails and long telephone calls. He'd already started studying for the California Bar.

He'd go back to Sierra Springs. Back to his girls. Jo would marry him. He knew that like he knew the lineup for tonight's game. It was just a matter of convincing her to trust him.

A chorus of "aahhhhs" around him pulled him out of his reverie. He looked at the field. Nothing had happened. At the scoreboard. A bank advertisement. Then he noticed everyone looking toward the aisle to his right.

"She's so cute!"

"Look at the hat!"

His gaze traveled with the comments, and fell on a two-foot-tall imp with curly black hair, giant soulful eyes and a pink Yankee baseball cap.

For a moment he couldn't think. He just stared across the seats at her, all the blood rushing to his thundering heart.

She reached out. "Cacacaca!"

He was almost afraid to take his eyes off her. She was a dream. A vision.

And holding her hand, another fantasy.

"I heard you have an extra ticket," Jo said, her beautiful mouth lifting into a smile, her own Yankee cap pulled low over her eyes. "And a lap for…my daughter."

In an instant, he'd jumped into the aisle and reached her in two strides.

"What are you doing here?" He put his arms on her shoulders and barely managed to keep himself from pulling her into him for a kiss he already tasted.

"I decided to meet you on your home turf." She glanced at the field. "Or grass, as the case may be."

He just shook his head, speechless, then looked down at Callie. "Is she walking?"

"She started about two weeks ago," Jo said with a laugh. "Remember Cam, Callie?"

He scooped her up and gently squeezed her. "Of course, she remembers me. She's my girl." He buried a kiss on her head, closing his eyes.

"She's one of your girls," Jo said softly.

He opened his eyes and met her gorgeous gaze. "Man, I don't think I've ever seen anything quite as awesome as you in a Yankee cap."

She touched the bill and they just looked at each other, grinning like a couple of fools.

"I can't believe you're here."

"Eddie remembered me," she said, glancing up toward the entrance. "And he promised me you were alone."

"Sit down, dude!"

He ignored the heckler and held Jo's gaze. "Why? What are you doing here, Jo?"

"I'm here because…because I…"

"Put the kid in a seat, buddy, we can't see the game!"

He wouldn't move. Couldn't move.

"Because I…" She tipped the hat back a little and looked hard at him. "I love you."

Air whooshed out of his lungs as he reached for her, hugging her and Callie together.

"Get a baby-sitter and a room, man! We're here to watch baseball."

She dipped out of his arms and glanced at the crowd. "Cam, let's sit down."

Grinning, he tugged her toward his box and guided

her into the empty seat next to his. Callie stood on his legs and looked behind him.

"No, sweetheart." He tried to turn her around. "The game's this way. See?"

Jo laughed. "I've been watching it on TV with her, but she doesn't quite get it."

"You've been watching baseball?" He looked at her in disbelief. "You didn't tell me that."

She nodded, reaching down between them to pick up his beer. "I got a satellite dish." She took a lusty sip and held the cup out to him. Casual. Like being in Yankee Stadium with a baby and a shared beer was an everyday occurrence. "I get every game, home and away."

His heart stuttered a few times. "No kidding."

"That way you can see the games."

Callie grabbed his ear, and he didn't even bother to disengage her. "When I'm visiting." That's what she meant, wasn't it? When he came to visit Callie.

She gave him a get-real look. "Yeah. When you're *visiting*. Mornings. Afternoons. Nights and weekends."

He shifted to face her, and Callie squirmed to get right between them. He inched his head to the side of her little body and snagged Jo's gaze again. "Could you clarify that for me, please?"

"Okay." Her smile was warm and real. "I love you, Cam. I want to marry you and spend the rest of my days and nights right next to you." She reached up and caressed his cheek. "Clear enough, counselor?"

Contentment washed over him. "Yeah. That's clear, tomgirl. That's perfect."

The crack of a high fly ball echoed into the night and fifty thousand fans shot to their feet and screamed.

Except for the two who preferred to kiss, with a baby between them.

Epilogue

Of all the McGrath men to find love over the past year, Cam never would have guessed that his dad would fall the hardest. Cam just shook his head and smiled as he watched the older man slow his gait enough to match the unstable strides of the toddler whose hand he held.

No doubt about it. Dad was a goner for Callie McGrath.

Cam leaned back in the oversize cane chair that looked out over the endless green lawn of Edgewater mansion. He inhaled the salty breeze that wafted off Rhode Island Sound and watched the hundred or so guests who danced, ate and celebrated at Colin and Grace's wedding reception.

"Look at those two," he said when Colin stepped onto the porch of the newly built Pineapple House Museum, his formal jacket and tie gone, his hair no longer bound in his signature ponytail.

Colin studied their father and Callie on the dance floor

set up under a giant yellow-and-white tent. "Yeah, I've been watching them. She might as well ask for the moon now, so he can put it on order for her next birthday."

Jim McGrath bent his gray head toward the tiny child to hear something that she babbled, then he stood straight and released a bellowing laugh.

"What could she have said to make him laugh so hard?" Cam asked his brother, both amused and amazed at the turn of events.

"Yeah, she only knows four words," Colin said. "Jo. Cam. Car and ball."

"The important stuff," Cam assured him, his gaze drifting across the dancers.

"I told you he's a different man," Colin said. "Like the weight of the world has been taken off his conscience."

But that hadn't been easy. Jim McGrath had to force himself to face each of his sons and apologize for decades of stubborn foolishness and deception. At first he tried to rationalize his behavior, then he owned up to his mistakes. He'd even flown to California for an emotional meeting with Jo and Callie.

With the past behind them, their mother and sister gone, the three brothers and the women they loved agreed to the only thing that made sense.

They forgave him. And ever since, their dad had appeared younger, happier and healthier than he had in years. And infatuated with his first grandchild.

From his vantage point on the elevated wraparound porch, Cam studied the dancers and the clusters of guests around the tables laden with food and champagne, searching for a glimpse of auburn hair and a flash of copper-penny eyes.

He hoped his wedding, scheduled for the following Christmas in Sierra Springs, would be just as glorious as this one. By then they'd have Katie's old salon entirely renovated into his new law offices, and he'd be ready to take the California Bar and start practicing law again, instead of running a massive legal department.

And, more important, their adoption of Callie would be finalized and she could add two more words to her repertoire: Mommy and Daddy.

"Have you seen Quinn?" Colin asked, taking a seat in the cane chair next to Cam.

"Behind you," Quinn said as he stepped through the front door of Pineapple House to join them. "Looking for the gorgeous woman I married and not you goons."

"You're stuck with us, bro," Colin said, nodding toward the far edge of the lawn where a balustrade enclosure lined the cliffs of the property. "Our women are bonding."

Grace, in her elegant, formfitting white gown, stood between Jo and Nicole, her arms around both their waists. Their heads were close as they exchanged confidences. Grace was telling them something, and Nic laughed, followed by Jo, the chiming sound dancing across the lawn just as the music stopped.

"What do you think they're talking about?" Colin asked.

"How lucky they are," Quinn joked.

The men laughed, but Cam couldn't resist stating the obvious. "As if they're the lucky ones."

Quinn crossed his arms and studied the group, no doubt his attention drawn to the dark-haired beauty he'd found in Florida. "You know, if it hadn't been for the hurricane that destroyed her resort, I'd have never found that woman," he said.

Colin nodded and indicated the building around them. "And if lightning hadn't struck Edgewater, who knows if Gracie and I would have ever met again and gotten past a ten-year-old misunderstanding?" As though she'd heard him, Grace looked toward the house, sending a blinding smile toward Colin, her blond hair shining in the sun, her green eyes full of love.

Cam studied the third woman in the group. In a slinky gold dress and heels, his tomgirl had been a show-stopper all day.

"And you found Jo after an earthquake," Quinn said slowly, his voice echoing the eerie chill that danced over Cam's skin.

The three men exchanged a look of astonishment at the realization.

"It seems we have a mother after all," Cam said with a quick laugh. "Mother Nature."

And she'd generously unleashed the power of earth, wind and fire to give them three lifetimes of love.

* * * * *

**Enjoy the launch of Maureen Child's
NEW miniseries**

THREE-WAY WAGER

*The Reilly triplets bet they could go
ninety days without sex. Hmmm.*

The Tempting Mrs. Reilly
by MAUREEN CHILD

(Silhouette Desire #1652)
Available May 2005

Brian Reilly had just made a bet to not
have sex for three months when his
stunningly sexy ex-wife blew into town.
It wasn't long before Tina had him
contemplating giving up his wager
and getting her back. But the tempting
Mrs. Reilly had a reason of her own
for wanting Brian to lose his bet…
to give her a baby!

Brenda Jackson

**and Silhouette Desire
present a hot new romance
starring another sexy
Westmoreland man!**

JARED'S
COUNTERFEIT
FIANCÉE

(Silhouette Desire #1654)

When debonair attorney
Jared Westmoreland needed a date,
he immediately thought of the beautiful
Dana Rollins. Reluctantly, Dana fulfilled
his request, and the two were somehow
stuck pretending that they were engaged!
With the passion quickly rising between
them, would Jared's faux fiancée turn
into the real deal?

Available May 2005 at your favorite retail outlet.

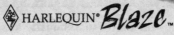

COMING NEXT MONTH

SDCNM0405